STEALER OF FLESH
KORMAK BOOK ONE

WILLIAM KING

Typhon Press Limited
GLASGOW, SCOTLAND

Copyright © 2012 by William King.

All rights reserved. No part of this publication may be reproduced, distributed or transmitted in any form or by any means, including photocopying, recording, or other electronic or mechanical methods, without the prior written permission of the publisher, except in the case of brief quotations embodied in critical reviews and certain other noncommercial uses permitted by copyright law.

Publisher's Note: This is a work of fiction. Names, characters, places, and incidents are a product of the author's imagination. Locales and public names are sometimes used for atmospheric purposes. Any resemblance to actual people, living or dead, or to businesses, companies, events, institutions, or locales is completely coincidental.

Book Layout ©2013 BookDesignTemplates.com

THE DEMON UNLEASHED

ALL AROUND THE unseasonal blizzard raged. Chill flakes of snow landed on Kormak's face. His feet felt numb, his clothing sodden. Hunger made his stomach growl. Cold leeched the strength from his limbs. He drew his cloak tight about his tall spare form but the wind still cut. He knew that he could not go much further and that he was doomed if he did not find shelter soon.

He pushed a strand of greying black hair from his eyes and squinted into the darkness. Night and snow made it difficult to see more than a few strides ahead.

He was not even sure he was on the road any more, the old route the Oathsworn Templars had taken to the Sacred Lands. The snow had piled up so he could not see the ancient flagstones the First Empire had placed here millennia ago. He was lost in this white wilderness.

This was not the way he had expected to die. When he had sworn his oaths as a Guardian he had thought he would fall in battle with some remnant of the Elder Races who had ruled the world before the coming of Men. There had been times when he had faced death by dark magic or beneath the curved obsidian scimitar of an orc. Once he had seen his end written in the eyes of a lovely vampire. He had not expected to pass in a way at once so terrible and so prosaic, to fall frozen where his brethren would have difficulty finding his body and recovering his dwarf-forged blade.

There should have been no snowstorms in eastern Belaria even this late in the autumn. The weather had been strange ever since the Great Comet had appeared in the sky. Perhaps it truly was a sign that the world was ending.

He wondered if it was worthwhile to continue leading his horse through the storm. There was a reason he was doing so but he could not remember what it was. It was as if the cold had frozen his mind as well as his body. Thinking was as difficult as putting one foot in front of the other.

Perhaps he should simply lie down and rest. Just for a moment, he could pillow his head in the soft snow drifts and gather his thoughts and his strength and then be on his way again. It would be good to rest . . .

No. That way lay death. If he stopped, he would never start again, would remain frozen in place until the spring thaws hit these vast plains. He would be covered by a blanket of snow which would not warm him but kill him. He needed to move and to keep moving.

And then what, a small, despairing part of his mind asked? What difference did it make? Soon he would reach the end of his strength. Soon his numbed limbs would fail and he would stumble and fall.

He remembered what he planned with the horse. He had heard once of a Kojar tribesman who had survived such a storm by slitting his horses belly and clambering inside it as a sleeping sack. He was not sure he believed that story and he doubted that it would work anyway, but what other hope did he have?

He raised his foot and put it down. Just keep going. One more step. And then another. He had been in worse situations. He had expected to die on other occasions and he was still alive. He needed to stay that way. He must succeed in tracking down the stolen amphora. The demon's prison could not be allowed to fall into the wrong hands. The ancient evil of the Ghul must not be allowed to enter the world once more.

He cursed. He had come so close back in Saladar. He had overtaken the thieves and almost caught them. Only one had escaped, carrying the sealed metal jar in which the Ghul had been bound, while the rest delayed him. He had killed them but they had bought time for the last to escape. If only he had been a fraction quicker he would already have been on his way back with the amphora and not stuck out here in this blood-chilling cold.

In the distance he heard howling. His horse, tired as he was, whinnied nervously. On these cold plains hunger sometimes drove the huge wolves to hunt men. They might be led by something worse. He had encountered sentient creatures who loved to hunt with the packs, had killed them when called upon to. There were tales of such creatures hunting in the Mountains of Darkness and those were not too distant. He must be close to the border of Belaria and Valkyria now. Maybe if the blizzard stopped he might even be able to see the peaks. Thinking of the wolves, he reached up to touch the blade that hung over his shoulder. His hands were so numb he felt only its outline in the air, not the texture of the thing.

The wind played strange tricks. It was difficult to tell how close the howling was. Would some huge grey form come loping out of the gloom just ahead or was the pack leagues away on the trail of something else? Almost he would have welcomed the fight. It would warm him up and if death came it would be quick and clean.

What was that? Ahead of him, just for a moment, through the flurries of snow, he thought he caught sight of a light. He told himself he was imagining it, that it was a product of his chilled imagination. There were no lights here. This was a place beyond all hope of human habitation, he was the last man alive on these cold plains. There was no light.

The howling sounded again, coming closer, he was sure. He trudged on, feeling as if he was moving up a rise. It was hard to tell, he had lost all sense of direction and orientation in the storm. From the way his legs felt, from the way he was coming close to stumbling, he was on a slope. Perhaps at the top of one.

There. Again. He saw a light. There was definitely something down there. Was he smelling smoke now or was that a trick of his imagination?

He thought about the wolves. He thought about the lights. It would be a cruel jest if the creatures pulled him down within sight of safety. He felt like laughing. He was assuming too much that he had been trained not to. There was no guarantee that the light represented safety. It could be a fire around which murderers sat or the creation of something far worse, intended to lure lost travellers to their dooms.

And yet would he be worse off if the creatures around the fire turned out to be killers, or things who wanted only to feast on his flesh and perhaps his soul? If they were men, he could fight them and take their fire, and if they were monsters . . . Well, he had been trained to kill such by those who were expert in the art.

He stumbled on and the light vanished; a cruel will o' the wisp sent to raise his hopes only to dash them. He kept moving in the direction he thought he had seen the light in, and he still thought he smelled smoke. His horse whinnied as if it too smelled safety. It began to push forward, moving in the same direction as Kormak and that reassured him; he was on the right trail. He let it drag him along in its wake.

The beast had lengthened its stride so that it was difficult for him to keep up. It was as much fleeing the wolves as it was moving towards what it thought might be a safe haven, and there was still the possibility that it might go wrong in the dark. Kormak stumbled and almost fell.

He knew now he was almost too weak to go on, and certainly too weak to face the wolves if they overtook him. He was at the end of his strength. All he could do was try to keep up with the horse and hope that it did not tug him off his feet. He was not sure he would ever rise again if that happened.

Ahead of them something large loomed out of storm and snow and night shadow, and blocked his progress. It took his frozen brain time to realise that it was a massive stone wall. He fumbled with his cold gauntleted hands and found no opening in it, so he started making his way around until he came to a gate. It was a large wooden one and it appeared to be closed. There was no way forward from where he was. He banged on it with his hands and shouted but he doubted there was any way he could be heard over the wind.

He laughed aloud. He had come so far only to be thwarted at the last. No. He would not give up. Gracelessly, he pulled himself into the saddle of his horse. The beast protested against his weight. It was just as tired as he was. No matter, he pulled on the reins and it reared. He gave it the command to kick and it brought its weight crashing down against the gate. He doubted the owners of this place would be too pleased by what he was doing but he had other concerns on his mind. The horse hammered the gate again and again but could not budge it. It seemed like the gateway had been built to withstand a battering ram. Kormak kept at it until the horse could do no more.

He slumped from the saddle, wearily, all of his energy gone. He thought he heard voices beyond the gate and tried to rise, but his limbs betrayed him. Dizziness swept over him and darkness took him.

He awoke in a bed. It was hard and lumpy but it was warm. He was inside in a room with wooden shutters and heavy drapes and a fire burning in one corner. Blankets and furs had been piled on top of him. The first thing he did was look around for his sword.

"Be still, stranger," said a wheezy old voice. "You are exhausted and you may well have suffered some damage at your extremities where the frosts spirits nibbled on your fingers and toes."

The accent was an odd one, but it spoke the trade tongue of the Holy Road understandably. Kormak looked up and saw a tall, skinny old man with a forked beard looking down on him. He had a candle on a plate in one hand. Many, many amulets dangled from his neck. All of them were covered in Elder Signs and mystic symbols; so were the dozens of rings on his fingers. A huge, armoured soldier in a surcoat with a rampant griffon stood behind him.

"Where am I?" Kormak asked.

"It is lamentable the clichés to which men resort in situations like this," said the old man in his wheezing voice.

"Are you going to answer my question or indulge in literary criticism?" said Kormak.

"You are in the mansion of Lord Tomas of Malaride," said the old man. Kormak kept his face carefully blank. Lord Tomas was the man who had sent the thieves to steal the amphora. It seemed he had stumbled into the place he was seeking. It was hardly surprising. It was where he had been trying to reach.

"Am I back on the Holy Road then?"

"You are lucky to be alive," the old man said.

"This I know," said Kormak. "How did I get here?"

"We heard the banging at the gate. Tarsus here insisted we investigate. He thought it might be orcs attacking," said the soldier. He was a massive man with a shaven skull that showed a lot of old scars. "A very nervous man is our friend Tarsus. For all his claims to be able to read the stars and see the future, he never foresaw it would be you and not orcs."

"Orcs have not been seen in these parts since the Nations went east at the end of the war," said Kormak.

"You know that. I know that. Apparently our scholarly friend here does not," said the guard.

"Be silent, Marcus," said the wizard. "You speak only to sneer at those more educated than you."

"Where is my sword?" Kormak asked.

"I trust you are not planning on using it on this wizened ancient. It would seem singularly ungrateful after he has saved your life," said Marcus.

"I have no reason to do that," said Kormak. Perhaps, he thought. Not yet.

"What are you doing in these parts?" The guard clearly knew something of the function of his order. "I have heard rumours that there are wolves that walk like men out there in the Mountains of Darkness. It seems the moondogs have rebelled against their liege lord, King Sturmbrand of Valkyria and those spawn of evil Lunar magic aid them. Do you seek them?"

"My sword. Where is it?"

Tarsus tipped his head to one side and inspected Kormak as if seeing him for the first time. "You are a Guardian of the Order of the Dawn," he said.

"I am."

"The Order of Assassins," the wizard added. His tone was a little hostile now.

"Such is not our function but I could understand why a wizard might see things that way."

"That's very generous of you," said Tarsus.

"I see you are intent on giving this ancient reprobate cause to regret using his healing herbs on you," said Marcus.

"If he has not broken the Law he has nothing to fear from me."

"You are not a very wise man, Guardian," said the guard captain.

"Most probably true," said Kormak, "and I have a feeling you are going to explain exactly why to me."

"You are still sick and weak and you are threatening the only man present who can heal you."

"I am threatening no one," said Kormak, "and only a fool would threaten me."

"He is correct, Marcus," said the wizard. "Those who kill Guardians rarely live long thereafter. His order is a most vengeful one and they have their ways of finding those who have done them wrong."

"It seems we have gotten off on the wrong foot," said Kormak. "I apologise for my tone and I thank you for your aid. You saved my life. I won't forget that."

The wizard coughed, covering his mouth with a white handkerchief. When it came away there was blood on it. He shrugged and looked almost guilty for a moment and then said, "You are welcome,

Guardian. I would have done the same for any man. If my words gave offence earlier, I apologise."

"My sword?" Kormak asked.

"You are determined," the guard said.

"His order live for those blades," said the wizard. "The worst sin he could commit would be to lose it."

The wizard coughed. "Your armour and your amulets and your weapons are in the keeping of Lord Tomas. As is your gold. It is all there. Nothing has been taken. Those artefacts are very valuable. Believe me Lord Tomas knows more about such things than most living men."

"What do I owe you?" Kormak said.

"Nothing," said the wizard. "As I said, I would have done the same for any man. Now you must take this herbal draught and rest, if you are to heal and regain your strength. I will not have all my healing undone by pleurisy and the wheezing death."

The two men rose to go. The wizard indicated the beaker and cup beside the bed. "Drink it," he said.

"I will do so," said Kormak, making his refusal clear. "But first I have much to think upon and prayers to make."

He did not want to say he was not going to be forced into drinking any potion by anyone, no matter how well disposed they seemed to be. There were some strange undercurrents here, he felt, although he was too tired to quite put his finger on what. Even as that thought occurred to him, the room seemed to spin. He clutched the bed and said nothing, determined not to let his weakness show. He did not want anyone to suspect how vulnerable he was.

If the men noticed anything, they said nothing, merely moved towards the door. Kormak was glad when they were gone.

Once the wizard had left, Kormak tried to rise. His head spun and he felt sick. Someone had placed a bowl beside the bed and he threw up into it. He realised he was cold and shivering and the room whirled.

The wizard had not lied when he had said Kormak was in a bad way. He had not felt this sick since he had taken an infected wound from an orc's scimitar. He staggered over to the window and moved the drapes. Outside all he could see was night and snow. The wind still howled down the chimney. He realised that he was very lucky indeed to still be alive.

He checked his fingers. There was no obvious frostbite damage, for which he was grateful. He was a man who lived or died by his skill with the sword.

He tottered over to the fire and stood there for a moment, warming himself. Someone had built it up to a blazing intensity and the heat on the front of his body made him aware of the chill on his back.

He stirred the fire anyway, enjoying the feel of the metal poker in his hands. He let it cool then he staggered back to place the metal rod on the table beside his bed. He inspected the alchemist's flask that sat beside the bowl. He unstoppered it, and allowed the smallest drop of its contents to fall on his finger. He sniffed, recognising the scent of bitterbloom and winterweed, two herbs used by chirurgeons the world over for the treatment of conditions such as his. He put his finger in his mouth and touched it with his tongue. He detected nothing amiss anyway, so he allowed himself to drink the smallest amount of the potion and waited to see if it had any effect.

Nothing untoward happened after fifteen minutes so he poured some of it into the bowl and drank it. He waited for another period and noticed some diminution of his fever and no other ill effects, so he drank the rest. He propped himself up on his pillows. He felt the potion begin to take effect and allowed himself to drop into sleep.

The stealthy opening of the door brought him instantly back to wakefulness. He opened his eyes narrowly and focused on the doorway. He did not move. In his weakened state he would need any edge he could get against the intruder and surprise was always the greatest of advantages. He saw a shadowy outline move closer across the room. Stealthily he grasped the poker. When the intruder reached the side of his bed, Kormak reached out and grabbed for the throat.

"You are awake then," said a woman's voice, surprisingly husky.

"Who are you?" Kormak said.

"You are as suspicious as they said."

"Probably more so," Kormak agreed. "You still have not answered my question, and I can assure you that your life depends on giving me a good answer."

"I am not a robber," said the woman. "I just wanted to take a look at the mysterious guest the storm deposited on our doorstep."

"Your name, lady. My patience is not limitless."

She laughed as if amused. "I am the Lady Kathea. I am the employer of the wizard who looked after you, or rather I am the wife of the man who employs him."

"And you decided to visit my room in the middle of the night to make sure of their handiwork?"

"I confess I was curious," she said. "I have never seen a Guardian before. I have read about them in the old tales, of course, but I have always thought they were legends. An order of knights sworn to oppose the Shadow, to protect humanity from the Old Ones. It seems more like a legend than something one would encounter in the light of day."

"My order is quite real, lady, and not nearly so heroic as the tales would have you believe."

"I am not surprised," she said. "Life is full of disappointments. Would you mind if I lit a candle? I am not quite so adept at seeing in the dark as you."

"Go ahead, but make no sudden movements."

She stepped away and went over to the fire. With a wooden spill she lit a candle and came back over to where Kormak sat. It was beeswax, not tallow, a sign that the lady or her husband were rich. Of course, he had not needed the candle to tell him that. The fact that they had a wizard in their retinue was evidence enough. She sat down in the same chair as the wizard Tarsus had. The candle underlit her face and he was not surprised to see that she was beautiful. Something about her voice, her movements and her confidence had already told him that she would be.

"You are quite lovely," he said, studying her golden hair, high cheekbones and large eyes.

"And you are very gallant for a monk."

"I am not a monk, lady. I am a soldier."

"And you fight a war against the Shadow."

"That is an overly dramatic way of putting it."

"I find it curious that you should appear out of nowhere at this time in this place. Why are you here? Who are you looking for?"

"I was looking for shelter from the storm."

Her head tilted to one side and he could tell she was studying him very carefully. "I cannot tell whether you are lying or not," she said at last.

"Why would I lie about such a thing?"

"Because you belong to an order that hunts men and wizards and other things and you are here now, of all times. It seems an odd coincidence."

"In what way?"

"I cannot believe you would be here, in the middle of this forsaken wilderness, for no reason."

"I was sent to recover something that was stolen, lady." He was not exactly sure why he was telling her this but he was tired and it was on his mind and he felt the need to talk. Perhaps it was the medicine and the illness.

"And perhaps to kill the one who ordered it so?" There was an edge to that question, an under-current of nervousness and anticipation. What had he stumbled into here, Kormak wondered.

"I have said too much already."

"No you have not. I bear you no ill will."

"I am very pleased to hear it." She leaned forward and without really knowing why, he reached up to move a strand of her hair that had fallen into her eyes. He was all too aware of the soft curves of her body. Kormak wondered why he was flirting with this woman. If she was, as she said, the wife of the local lord it was a very dangerous thing to do. Of course, that might have been part of its attraction. And there was the situation. It was night. They were in his room. He was affected by the medicine he had taken earlier.

"You are not what I expected at all," she said. Her voice was soft and thoughtful.

"What did you expect?"

"A fanatic and a killer."

"A killer I am, lady. One who wonders why you felt the need to visit him alone in the dark."

She seemed about to say something then shook her head. "I do not think I am any wiser than when I came in but I shall deny you your rest no longer, Guardian."

She rose from the chair and went to the door, taking her candle with her. When she left the room, more light than its went with her. Kormak lay awake in the darkness for a long time, listening to the wind howl, watching the fire die. Tired as he was, sleep would not come. At some point he thought he heard a scream but it might have been the wind or it might just have been the edge of a dream intruding into the world.

The wind still howled outside when Kormak woke. He rose from the bed and tottered to the window, throwing aside the curtains. Outside it was day but the snow storm made it hard to make out any details. He saw flakes falling hard and fast into a courtyard and beyond that he thought he saw a high stone wall. It was obvious he was in a fortified manor of some sort and quite a large one. His head felt fuzzy and vague and he still felt weak. Someone had come in through the night and put more wood on the fire. It alarmed him that he had not woken. Normally he slept lightly and the faintest noise would wake him. He was in worse shape than he thought.

He moved back towards the bed as he heard footsteps in the corridor. He was sitting upright as Tarsus entered. The wizard looked even older in the daylight. His face was deeply lined, etched with marks of pain. Crow's feet made trenches around his eyes. His hair was a dirty grey. The whites of his eyes were yellowish. Kormak noticed that his nails were long in the manner of the eastern aristocracy, a scholarly caste who liked to show they did not need to perform manual labour, or even wield a blade.

"You have made a better recovery than I expected," Tarsus said. "You must be a very strong man."

Kormak looked at him. "You have come to check up on me?"

"I have. It would do my reputation no good for me to save you from the effects of cold, only to die of something else."

"Your reputation is important to you?"

"You don't like wizards, do you, Guardian? I suppose that is understandable."

"I have seen too much evil worked by wizards."

"We have no monopoly on wickedness, sir."

"That is nothing less than the truth."

The wizard raised one bushy grey eyebrow. "I am surprised to hear you admit it."

"Only a fool denies what his eyes can see," Kormak said.

"Sometimes what we see is an illusion."

"We were doing so well there, wizard. We had found a point of agreement and you have to go and spoil it by your allusions."

Tarsus smiled. "It was illusions I mentioned but we shall forget that. Let me see your hands."

"They are quite functional."

"Nonetheless I would like to inspect my work."

Kormak extended his hands carefully. He knew of a great deal of inimical magic that could be worked by touch and he was not wearing his amulets or carrying his blade and he was still not sure how trustworthy any of these people were. The wizard took his hands and turned them over. He squinted as he inspected them. His touch felt cold.

"Very good," he said at last. "No permanent damage. You will be able to wield a sword with what I assume will be your customary proficiency."

"Do you expect me to have to anytime soon?"

"An odd question, Guardian."

"I have been asked a few odd questions since I arrived." The wizard tilted his head to one side. The amulets on his neck jingled together. "By whom?"

"By yourself. Among others."

"This is an isolated place, people are naturally curious."

"I am surprised to find a wizard so far from the haunts of men."

"Why? Did you think your order had killed all of them in the area?"

Kormak wondered if Tarsus and the Lady Kathea had talked. "It is strange that a scholar should choose to live so far from the great cities and libraries."

"You are one of those that think wizards only avoid the haunts of men if they have something to hide."

"The thought had crossed my mind."

"And a very suspicious mind it is, I can see. I suppose that is only natural for a man in your profession."

"Why do you dwell here?"

"I shall have to show you my patron's library and his collection once you are well, then perhaps you will understand."

"Your patron?"

"Lord Tomas is a collector of ancient artefacts and a considerable scholar in his own right."

"Will I be meeting him any time soon?"

"You seem fit enough to be allowed out of bed so I am guessing yes. You will most likely be invited to dine with us."

Kormak stared hard at the wizard. The old man met his gaze with rheumy eyes. He coughed and once more his lips were speckled with blood. He noticed Kormak looking.

"I have more trouble healing myself than others," he said. He got up and limped to the door. He stared at Kormak. "I am not the one you are looking for," he said. "No matter what you think."

The door closed behind him. Kormak heard it being locked.

Servants brought Kormak clean, warm clothing. It seemed to have been made for a man his height but somewhat larger about the waist. A servant showed him through the manor to the dining hall. Two men at arms accompanied them. Both looked competent and both were armed and armoured and they watched him closely. He suspected there were others within easy call.

The place was larger than he had thought. Corridors ran in many directions and the architectural style belonged to the First Empire, all clean simple lines, not the more ornate gargoyle and Elder Sign encrusted work favoured by those who ruled the West in this age of the world. The place was vast and echoing and seemed half-empty. He saw servants and men at arms moving about, enough so that they would have seemed a decent sized retinue for a mid-ranking nobleman in the west. Here they seemed to be lost in the vast draughty space.

All the retainers had a griffon on their tunics and griffon banners adorned the walls. It was worked into some of the ancient stonework too which suggested that either Lord Tomas's family had been here for a very long time, or possibly more likely, they had taken their heraldic emblem from the iconography of their mansion.

The servant showed him into a huge hall that contained many tables only one of which was occupied. That table, like the others, was large enough to seat scores but there was only four people there, all clustered at the top of the table, where a bard also stood clutching a harp.

He knew three of the people; Tarsus and Lady Kathea and another man, garbed as a wandering mercenary knight. He clearly recognised Kormak. This was one of the thieves Kormak had been sent to hunt down. He had managed to escape back in Saladar. He glared at Kormak. The Guardian was very aware that the man was armed and he was not. The aristocrat at the head of the table must be Lord Tomas. He was a tall, stately looking man, silver-haired and still fit. He had the authority and the manner of a nobleman at his own hearth.

Lady Kathea met his gaze for a moment, flushed slightly then looked away. Kormak wondered what was going on here.

All of them rose, in the courtly, old-fashioned way of country nobles greeting a visitor. All of them bowed and Lord Tomas introduced them all in formal Hardic. The thief was called Wesley here. After the introductions were made, they all sat down while an array of servants brought food and wine.

"Play something for us, Ivan," Lord Tomas said, and the bard struck up a tune. He played softly and very well. It was a tune Kormak had heard played at the court of King Brand when the elderly wanted to hear a tune popular in their youths.

"You are from Taurea, Sir Kormak," Lord Tomas said.

"Aquilea, sir," Kormak replied. He wondered when they would get to the real business of the evening. With Wesley present there could be no doubt Lord Tomas knew who he was and why he was here.

"I thought you were not a Sunlander. Your order has its home in Taurea though, the fortress-monastery on Mount Aethelas."

"That is so," said Kormak.

"There are chapter houses in all the Northern Kingdoms," said Tarsus. "And once a long way beyond. They say the reach of your order is much diminished now although your presence here would seem to prove that wrong." There was a note of satisfaction in his voice.

Kormak looked at them all. He had a feeling of being hemmed in by enemies. There were guards around the chamber and everyone except him was armed. He was still physically very weak. It seemed impossible that Lord Tomas did not know why Kormak had come. And yet, so far, no one had threatened him. He had been healed and treated with courtesy. It was not what he had expected at all.

"Kormak. It seems to me I have heard that name before," said Lord Tomas. "A member of your order distinguished himself in the Orc Wars. As I recall a highlander of that name saved the life of King Brendane. Was that you?"

"I was there. I helped defend the King. I did not do it on my own."

"That is not the way the tales tell it. The way the bards sing of it, you were found standing atop a mountain of orc corpses guarding the wounded King."

"I was the only survivor of those guarding him at the time. The poets exaggerate the rest."

"I wonder," said Wesley. "There are other tales attached to the name, not all of them pleasant ones."

Lord Tomas made a small, curt chopping gesture with his hands. "Now, Wesley, let us have no unpleasantness at our table. You are all my guests. I would have us all be friends while we are within my hall."

Wesley smiled. It was not a pleasant smile. Kormak studied him closely. He was a powerfully built man, with very pale skin, which his jet black hair, beard and brows made seem all the more pale. His manner was lazily confident.

"I was wondering as to the nature of your association," said Kormak. "How is it that two such disparate individuals know each other?"

It was time to start getting to the bottom of the mysteries here. Lord Tomas looked from Kormak to Wesley and seemed to come to a decision.

"I am a collector, Sir Kormak. I come from a line of collectors. My grandfather started our collection. My father enlarged it and passed it on to me and I have done my humble best to curate and extend it."

There was real enthusiasm in the older man's manner.

"What do you collect?" Kormak asked.

"Ancient artefacts. Old books. Objects of mystical significance from all over the world. We have cloaks woven by the Old Ones. I have a library of First Empire tomes and scrolls, all written in High Solari. I have amulets and wands and staves from the Elder world. A runestone said to belong to the Wizard-King Solareon. I have weapons and armour forged by the dwarves when they still did work for men. You possess some very fine examples of those yourself, I could not help but notice when you were brought through my gate."

"It sounds fascinating."

"I understand your order maintains a similar such library at Mount Aethelas. I pride myself that my own collection may some day come to rival it."

"A worthy goal," Kormak said.

"My husband has spent a fortune acquiring new samples for his collection," said Lady Kathea. She did not sound at all pleased by this. A frown marred her lovely face. She ran a long-nailed finger over her full lips.

"Fortunately, my dear, I have a fortune," said Lord Tomas. "My family own extensive estates all through eastern Belaria and my factors have proven to be merchants of superlative skill. They have done nothing but multiply the wealth I inherited. I can afford to indulge my passions."

"We have not asked, Sir Kormak, what business brings him to this part of the world," said Tarsus. His tone was sour. His smile malicious. It seemed that he too wanted to bring things out into the open. "Are you hunting someone, Guardian, or do you seek some deadly monster that has broken the Law."

"I was sent to reclaim something that was stolen," said Kormak, fixing his eyes on Wesley. "An ancient artefact as coincidence would have it. It was dredged from the World Ocean off the Sundown Islands by a fisherman and came into the hands of the Museum Keeper in Tanaar. He recognised it for what it was and sent to my order for someone to dispose of it. While I was en route, the museum was robbed and the Keeper murdered. The thieves fled with what they had taken."

"And what was that," Lord Tomas asked. There was a strange glitter in his eyes.

"An ancient amphora from the time of the Emperor Solareon. In it was bound a Ghul, one of the demons sometimes known as the Stealers of Flesh."

"Why would anyone want such an object?" Lady Kathea asked. She was staring hard at her husband. Kormak sensed animosity there.

Kormak looked from Wesley to Tarsus to Tomas. He let his gaze rest on each one in turn. "I don't know. The thing imprisoned within the amphora is a very dangerous creature, a peril to both body and soul."

"I believe that is merely a matter of opinion," said Lord Tomas.

"It is more than that I can assure you," said Kormak. "The demons are all but unkillable without specially forged runic weapons. They are bodiless, restless evil spirits. To live they must possess the bodies of new victims every few days or weeks. The Emperor Solareon bound them into amphorae. After his death, his successor Justin the Holy, repulsed by the thought of such things being stored in his palace, ordered the jars to be thrown into the deepest part of the ocean. It was a cursed day when this one showed up in that fisherman's nets. The thieves that took it made a very grave mistake."

"Did they, Sir Kormak?" Lord Tomas asked. There was a cold smile on his face. Kormak decided he wanted to end this charade now.

"One of the thieves fell from the wall when he left the museum. His leg was broken. His companions abandoned him. He fell into the hands of the local magistrate who was not gentle. Under torture he gave a description of his confederates and the name of the man who employed him."

"Did he now?" Lord Tomas said. He seemed more amused than threatened.

"I overtook the thieves on the road, in Saladar. Only one of them escaped me. The strangest thing is, I see him sitting at this table." He pointed a finger at Wesley.

"And I suppose the thief claimed that I was the man who employed him," said Lord Tomas.

"He did, sir," said Kormak.

"He did not lie," said the nobleman.

"I never for a moment thought so," said Kormak.

"Well that has certainly cleared the air," said Tarsus. He coughed. Blood speckled his lips. He wiped it away with a napkin. The gesture was surprisingly delicate.

"I am surprised you are taking the news so calmly," said Kormak. He studied the table. There was a knife there intended for carving meat. It was not much of a weapon but it was better than none at all.

"Obviously it is not news," said Lord Tomas.

"You won't get away with it," said Kormak. "If you kill me my order will send more to avenge me. They always do."

"Come, Sir Kormak," said Tarsus. "If anyone here meant you ill, we could simply have left you to die in the snow. I would not have wasted my herbs on you if I had sought to do you harm."

The wizard, in particular, seemed to want to let Kormak know he was innocent of any evil intention.

"You are my guest," said Lord Tomas. "You have eaten my food, taken my salt. No harm will come to you here unless you try to harm us. On this I give my word." He looked pointedly at Wesley as he said this.

"Then I am confused," said Kormak. "Do you intend to return the amphora and pay restitution to the families of the men who were killed?"

"No, Sir Kormak, I do not. I do however have a proposition I would like to put to you. We can discuss it after dinner while we look at this ancient artefact you have come so far to recover."

"Well, what do you think?" Lord Tomas asked. He gestured at the amphora emphatically. It clearly had pride of place in his huge collection. Kormak looked around. He was reminded of the Museum in Tanaar. There was the same huge array of shelves with scrolls and alembics and crystal jars on them. A suit of gold-embossed runic armour, the complete war-gear of a Solari Centurion rested on a stand in one corner. There was the skeleton of some gigantic beast, a dragon perhaps, that had been reassembled and stood in one corner. Kormak wondered if his sword and the rest of his equipment were here. The place was certainly secure enough. Lord Tomas had triple-locked the massive metal doors that were the only entrance.

Tomas looked from Kormak and back to his latest prize. Kormak noticed the eyes of all the others were upon him. Tarsus watched him closely, Wesley with malice in his eyes. Lady Kathea had withdrawn to her chambers, not part of the conspiracy or perhaps that was what they wanted him to think.

He moved closer to the object and inspected it.

It looked like a simple metal alembic, made from lead. It was inscribed with Elder Signs and stoppered with a plug of truesilver. The plug was sealed with metal, soldered shut. There was writing on the side. Kormak recognised one of the seals on the side of the flask and he could decipher the inscription. In part it was a name; Razhak. He suspected that he was far from the only person in the room who could do that.

"This is an evil thing," he said, at last. Lord Tomas's eyes were feverishly bright.

"Then you think it is one of the Binding Flasks of King Solareon. As I do."

"It is difficult to be sure without performing certain tests," Kormak said. Lord Tomas picked up the flask and handled it as another man might handle a baby.

"I would not do that if I were you," Kormak said. "There is a taint in that thing that might leak out and affect you."

Lord Tomas put it back on the marble counter-top and placed the crystal shield on top of it once more. "You can see why I am excited, can't you?" He spoke as if this was the most reasonable thing in the world to say, and Kormak began to wonder about his sanity, about the sanity of all the people present in this vast sepulchral chamber.

"I am not sure excitement is the correct emotion to feel," Kormak said. "Dread would perhaps be more appropriate."

"Come now, Sir Kormak," said Lord Tomas. "Surely a man of your order is not afraid. I have always heard the Guardians of the Dawn enjoyed the special protection of the Holy Sun. Of all of us, you have the least to worry about from the contents of that flask."

"There is a demon in it," Kormak said. "A demon of a particularly potent sort; one that was bound by Solareon more than a millennium ago."

Lord Tomas looked at him. "There is a Ghul confined in that bottle, Sir Kormak. I would not call it a demon in the sense that most people would understand the word."

"It is immortal, inimical to Men and will perform acts of the greatest wickedness if freed," said Kormak. "I would say that fits most people's understanding of what a demon is."

"But you and I know differently. The Ghuls were once men like us," said Lord Tomas.

Kormak shook his head. "They were servants of the Old Ones who rebelled against them but they were not men."

"They were mortals then, and they seized the secret of immortality from their masters."

Kormak thought he began to understand the cause of Lord Tomas's excitement and the direction this conversation was going to take. "We do not know that for certain," Kormak said. "We know only what the Sage Cronas wrote."

"But Cronas sat at the right hand of Solareon, and Solareon was the greatest wizard who ever lived."

"All the more reason not to trifle with his work."

"Your blade could destroy a Ghul, could it not, Sir Kormak?"

"Is that what you would have me do?"

"Eventually, yes," said Lord Tomas.

"But first you have questions to ask of the monster," said Kormak. "Questions concerning the nature of its immortality and how it might be achieved."

"Exactly so," said Lord Tomas.

"We already know how the Stealers of Flesh achieved their immortality," said Kormak. "They take possession of the bodies of other living things and consume their life force. They are vampires of a most awful sort."

"Yes but in the Codicils to the Deed of Solareon Cronas writes that it was not always so. That the Ghul sought the same form of immortality as the Old Ones and that something went wrong with the process. Cronas sat with his master while Solareon questioned the bound demons."

"Then you have read works by the Sage that my teachers never did," said Kormak.

"Your order had no monopoly on ancient knowledge, Guardian," said Lord Tomas. "There are far more books in the world than exist even in the library at Aethelas. I have some of them on my shelves here."

"And some of them are filled with traps set to lure men to their doom," said Kormak.

"Spoken like a true witch-finder," said Tarsus.

"I have had experience of such things, have you?" Kormak said.

"That is why we want you with us," said Lord Tomas. "With your knowledge and your blade there will be no missteps. We will be able to question the demon in safety."

"You think I will help you learn how to transform yourselves into Stealers of Flesh? That is insane," said Kormak. He could not keep his true thoughts hidden. The words were torn from him.

"You misunderstand our intentions, Sir Kormak," said Tarsus. "We seek no such thing."

"Tarsus speaks the truth," said Lord Tomas. "We seek to learn what the demon knows, that is true, but we also seek to learn what went wrong. The Ghul must possess a fantastic amount of knowledge. It may put us on the path to immortality. We can learn where they went wrong, avoid their errors and perhaps all men will be able to live forever."

There was total compelling belief in his voice. Kormak realised to his astonishment that the nobleman meant every word he was saying. He was quite sincere, and possibly quite mad.

"I do not think that is possible," said Kormak.

"But the Ghuls did," said Tomas. "And they went more than halfway towards achieving it. Think of the possibilities, Sir Kormak. I mean really think of them. Think what might be achieved here."

All of them were watching him closely and it came to him then that any refusal on his part might have fatal consequences. They would not want him free to oppose them, if he turned them down. At this moment in time, weak as he was, he was sure he could overcome a wizard and an ancient nobleman. Wesley might prove more of a problem. And then what? He would be sick and trapped in the mansion having committed murder. Kormak wondered if he should play along at least until he got his weapons back. Something of his doubts must have showed in his face, for the nobleman looked at him sidelong.

"I do not think what you wish to do is possible," said Kormak. He knew they had seen his doubts earlier and he doubted he could convince them he had suddenly changed his mind. Perhaps, if he seemed to be convinced . . .

A wintery smile flickered across Lord Tomas's face. "You may be right, Sir Kormak. You may be. But what if you are not? This could be the eve of the greatest discovery ever made by men. If you are wrong, all of our names will ring down the ages, even yours, for you will be part of this thing."

"You intend to free a demon bound by Solareon," said Kormak. Even if he was going to pretend to let them convince him, he was going to make them fight for it. "They were imprisoned for a reason."

"Even Solareon interrogated them and he did that too for a reason. They have much lost knowledge. Much knowledge that men have never possessed at all."

"And Solareon found nothing," Kormak said. He kept his voice calm. "He learned nothing. What makes you think you can succeed when the greatest wizard in history failed?"

"Because great as he was Solareon did not possess the sum total of all wisdom. We have learned new things. We have parts of the puzzle he did not. Given time we could be greater even than Solareon. Or are you one of those men who think our ancestors were titans who could never be exceeded? I can assure you they were not. They were men just like us. Even Solareon. I have studied their works enough to know."

"Don't you see that if you unleash this creature it will work terrible evil on the world?"

"If we unleashed it uncontrolled, that might well be the case. But we have the means to compel it. We have your sword, a thing that Solareon did not. We have the means to end its life, a weapon that will prove inevitably fatal to the Ghul if we use it. It will obey us or it will die. And there is your answer, Sir Kormak. If we succeed, we triumph. If we fail, we will kill it and there will be one less demon free in the world. Even you cannot object to that."

"I need time to consider," said Kormak.

"Promise me you will think about what I have asked," said Lord Tomas reaching out and clutching Kormak's arm. His grip was surprisingly strong. His eyes glittered. Kormak realised there was more than just excitement in his manner. He was afraid. Given what he was contemplating, that was only natural. "But we have kept you too long. It is late and you must retire and regain your strength. You will need it soon."

One way or another he was right, Kormak thought.

When he heard the strange knock, Kormak rose grasped the poker and walked over to the door. He unbarred the door and was not entirely surprised to see the Lady Kathea standing there. She had a night-light in her hand.

"May I come in?" she asked. Her hair was unbound. There were traces of cosmetics on her face. The pupils of her eyes seemed very large and reflected the light she held.

"This is your home." She took that as an assent and walked by him, close enough so that he could smell her perfume. The fabric of her long dress brushed against him as she walked. She went over to the fire and stood beside it.

"So they have asked you to help them?" she said.

"Lady?"

She turned and looked at him over her shoulder. "They have asked you to help them with the ancient prison they have found. The one with the demon in it."

Kormak just looked at her, not sure where this was going. She spoke to fill the silence as he had known she would.

"I am curious. Will you help them? Are you tempted?"

"How do you know what your husband seeks?"

"Because he is my husband. I know what he dwells upon. I know his obsessions. I know the books of poetry he reads. I know what he dreams of. He was not the sort of man who would seek glory on a battlefield but this represents glory of another sort."

"You think he wants glory?"

"I think he dreams a dream that has been dreamt by others in the past, never to good effect."

"You do not approve?"

"At first I thought it was a fancy, like many of his others. He has developed some obsessions in the past, Sir Kormak. With alchemy, with ancient books and lore. I can see now that all of those obsessions led him to this. I never really expected it to go anywhere. But then his agents located that flask and the wizard and he seems determined to go ahead with his plan."

"And you think I should help him?"

"I think he will proceed whether you help him or not."

"I sense you do not approve of this."

"It is madness, Sir Kormak. Surely you can see this? The others, they do not. They are all caught up in it. Lord Tomas can be a very persuasive man. We are in a world where he commands everything and a long way from anywhere else. This place has its own deceptive reality. It swallows you up, devours all common sense if you stay long enough."

"Except in your case, apparently."

She smiled sadly. "You don't believe me?"

"I am wondering why you have chosen to confide your doubts in me, so soon after the matter was discussed with your husband. It seems a trifle convenient."

"You are a very suspicious man."

"Being so has helped keep me alive."

"I am sure that is the case, given the life you lead."

"I will not be allowed to leave here alive if I do not aid your husband. Telling you I planned not to help him would undoubtedly shorten my life."

"You think I will report what you say to my husband? Is that what you think?" There was anger in her voice. She moved closer to him, looked up into his eyes. Their bodies were almost touching.

"Won't you?" She swallowed but her face was calm. Her lips were slightly parted. With her head held back he could not help but notice the way her hair tumbled down her back.

"I doubt it would make much difference. My husband has given his word not to harm you and I am sure he will keep it."

"Telling me anything different would be foolish."

"You do not know Tomas like I do. He is a man who keeps his word. Even if he was not, he fears the vengeance of your order. A man who plans to live forever would be foolish to court the enmity of an organisation with the will and the power to terminate his unending existence."

"People are rarely so logical when they are afraid."

"My husband is."

"You are saying that if I tell him I would not help, he will let me go?"

"I said he would not kill you. I suspect he would hold you here until he has achieved his goal. I also think he would borrow the use of your sword and your amulets. My husband is a bold man in his own way, and a wealthy one, and he is used to getting his way."

There was something in the way she said it that made him realise she resented her husband very much. He suspected that she was probably telling him the truth as she saw it as well.

"You know this and you think I should try and stop him?"

"I have read of Solareon and his war with the Ghul. That flask was sealed for a reason. You know that and I know that. Tomas knows it too. He just chooses to ignore it because he believes he is immune to the consequences that normal mortals must face. And why should he not? For all of his life he has been."

"Let us, for the sake of argument, assume that I believe you. How am I supposed to stop your husband, when I am weak and he has a keep full of men at arms, and a sorcerer at his disposal? I suspect your husband has some skill in that field as well."

"Tarsus is old and weak and not long for this world."

"All the more reason for him to seek the secrets of immortality. He is in desperate need of them. He wants what that amphora can give him."

"Wanting something and having the strength to seize it are two different things," she said. She let her dress slip from her shoulder. She was naked beneath and very beautiful. She moved closer. Her breasts flattened against his chest. She put a finger on his lips. He reached forward and grabbed her lush hair with his fist and twisted. She stood on her tip-toes, a faint moan emerged from her parted lips. She simply looked into his eyes knowingly.

He threw her on the bed and pushed his weight down on top of her. She welcomed him willingly.

"Why do you hate your husband?" Kormak asked, as they lay naked on the bed. She smiled at him lazily.

"Is that what you think this is about?"

"Isn't it?"

She looked away. The fire had died down. "In part, I suppose. My husband bought me from my brother, in return for my brother's position as his factor. I was just another thing he collected and then lost interest in. Now I am here, in this isolated place, where no one knows me or respects me, with a man whose indifference is worse than dislike. I am a prisoner here, Sir Kormak, in much the same way as you are."

"So you admit I am a prisoner."

"You will be treated with every courtesy but you will not be allowed to leave until you have done what my husband requires."

"You said he fears the enmity of my order."

"We are a long way from Mount Aethelas and your order will not investigate unless you die or are a long time returning. Is that not so?"

Kormak nodded. "You have no weapons and your horse will be found to be lame. Reasons will be given to put off your departure. Unless you force the matter, you will not be physically restrained."

"And if I give your husband the help he seeks?"

"Are you tempted to?" She sounded worried.

"Your husband is a rich man. He might reward me well for his help. By the Sun, he might make me immortal."

"You don't really think that is possible, do you?"

"It may be."

"And you would help my husband free a demon in order to gain its knowledge?" She looked at him angrily. Again, she seemed sincere.

"It is something I need to consider."

She turned to face him. The length of her naked body pressed against his. "You are a very cautious man. You still don't trust me, do you?"

Kormak shrugged. "I don't trust anybody."

"Not even yourself, it seems."

The door burst open. Lord Tomas was there. Wesley was beside him and a number of men at arms. They looked ready to use their weapons at the slightest provocation. Naked and unarmed, Kormak did not fancy his chances against them.

"I came to ask your decision," Lord Tomas said. He looked from Kormak to his wife. "I heard you . . . talking to my wife."

Kormak said nothing. There was nothing to say. He could tell that behind his cold facade, Lord Tomas was incandescent with rage.

He glanced at Wesley and his men at arms who studiously kept their faces blank, to avoid admitting they had noticed his humiliation.

"Take Sir Kormak to the dungeon," he said. He strode forward and grasped Kathea roughly with the arm.

"You and I will have words, wife," he said.

The guards surrounded Kormak, weapons drawn. There was nothing he could do except throw himself on their blades and he doubted that would do anybody much good.

Wesley tossed him his clothing. There was a smirk on his face now that the eyes of Lord Tomas were no longer upon him. "I think Lord Tomas has decided he no longer has need of your services."

The cell was cold and damp and the bars were strong. Kormak had tested them and they resisted his strength. He cursed his own stupidity and the weakness that illness had brought. Somewhere in the mansion, a conspiracy of maniacs were going to unleash a demon, and he doubted that any of them had any real idea of what that meant. Kormak was not sure that even he did. No one had encountered a Ghul in hundreds of years since the Guardian Malos had hunted down the last of them. It had left a trail of death and mayhem hundreds of leagues long once it had been uncovered.

He grabbed the bars again and shook them but they would not give. One of the guards said, "That won't do you much good. Man can't bend iron that thick. Believe me."

It was Marcus, the guard who had been there when Tarsus first treated him. There were three other men sitting at the table, playing cards.

"Your master is going to unleash a demon," Kormak said.

"He told me you were suffering from delusions," said the guard, "and needed to be restrained for your own good till you got better. I can see he wasn't wrong."

Kormak studied the man. He had keys on his belt. If he could lure him close enough he might be able to knock the man out and get the keys and free himself. And then he would only need to overcome three armed men, he thought sourly. After that he would find Lord Tomas and then what, he asked himself? The ritual would be guarded. Lord Tomas had clearly thought things out. Still, he would worry about that after he was free. He considered faking illness but he doubted that would put the jailor within reach.

These were cautious men and strong. He was not going to be able to fight his way out of here.

There was a sound of knocking from the door at the head of the stairs leading down into the cells. The jailor walked over and looked out through a slot. He said something and nodded and opened the door. Kormak looked up and saw the wizard Tarsus. The old man limped down the stairs, walked over to the table where the guards sat and helped himself to some of their wine. None of them objected. He seemed to have some trouble fumbling the stopper back on the jug. It took him some time to get in place then he came over to the cell door and looked at Kormak.

"You could have handled this better," said Tarsus. His tones were very low.

"Have you come to gloat?" Kormak asked.

"No," he said.

"Shouldn't you be helping Lord Tomas free the Ghul?"

"I should be but I am not. I told him I was too sick."

"Why did you come here?" Kormak asked.

"I came to help you," Tarsus said. "It was one thing to talk about unleashing the Ghul when it was just a theoretical possibility. It is a different thing entirely since I have held the amphora in my hands. I can feel the evil in the thing. I want no part in setting it free."

"Not even if it can help you stave off death?" Kormak asked.

"I doubt it can do that now. There is not enough time left for me to learn its secrets and even if there was, I am not sure I would seek immortality at such cost."

"But you thought differently once."

"Like I said, contemplating a thing in theory is different from putting it into practise. And I am old and tired and I will rest in my grave." He coughed again and more blood came up. "I have not found life so much to my taste that I look forward to prolonging it."

"How can you help me?" Kormak asked.

Tarsus glanced over at the jailors. They lay slumped over the table, heads down, exceedingly drowsy. Tarsus walked over to the head jailor and took the keys.

"Why are you doing this?" Kormak asked.

"I am a man no worse and no better than yourself, Sir Kormak. I do not want to see that demon unleashed and I believe that between us, we might stop that from happening."

"I am still not entirely sure I can trust you."

The wizard unlocked the cell. "Well, when you make up your mind, perhaps you will follow me to Lord Tomas's vault. I suspect I will prove slightly less impressive with a blade than you but I'll do what I can."

Kormak pushed the door of the cell. It swung open. He stepped through warily. Tarsus had already turned his back and was limping over to the stairs. He did not seem to care that Kormak was in a position to bludgeon him down. Kormak walked over to the jailors. They were still breathing. He helped himself to one of their blades and their heavy leather jerkins. It would do no harm to have a disguise as they moved through the manor house.

"They are not dead," said Tarsus. "It was just a sleeping powder added to their wine. I used to play chess with Marcus. I rather like him."

"Any treachery, wizard, and I'll cut you down."

"Then how will you find your way to the Sanctum? Ask the guards?"

"You have an answer for everything, don't you?"

"I find one of the few good things about old age is that it's given me enough experience to cover most situations."

"There's no need to sound so smug about it."

"I take my pleasures where I can find them."

"Is that another piece of wisdom that occurred to you in your decrepitude?"

"You'll be old too one day, Guardian, if you are lucky. I hope you encounter another soul as miserable as yourself then."

"Well, you've given me some answers for them, haven't you?"

"Glad to be of service."

Tarsus hobbled up the stairs; Kormak followed him out into the huge ancient manor. It was dark and cold and the wind howled.

They moved across the courtyard and for the first time Kormak got a really good look at the outside of the manor. It was massive, an ancient palace that sprawled across the hilltop. Most of it had a half-ruined look to it, was covered in winter ivy and other creepers. There was a fountain in the courtyard with no water in it. The central statue was of a mermaid with dragon-spines running down her back. It was an odd thing to see so far from the sea.

"They are in the crypts below the mansion," Tarsus said. "Lord Tomas is going to perform the ritual."

"Why are you not there? Won't they suspect something?"

"I told them I was too ill to take part. It was not hard to make them believe that."

Suspicion stabbed at Kormak again. He wondered whether he was being led into some sort of complex trap. He could not see how it would work when it would have been easy enough for Lord Tomas to have him trussed up and brought to the catacombs. That did not mean it was not possible though. He had known of Old Ones who liked to play strange games with the minds of their victims. Perhaps these men were like that.

Tarsus picked an archway in the side of one tumbled down building. There were strange signs carved into the stonework of the lintel. They resembled no Elder Sign that Kormak knew of.

The old man paused for a moment. He was shivering. "At least we are out of the wind," he said. "It chills me right to the bone these days."

"That may be the least of your worries soon," Kormak said. Tarsus nodded and fumbled in an alcove in a wall. He produced a torch which he smeared with some sort of sulphur paste. With a word of power, he lit it. An infernal stench filled the air.

"You can still work sorcery, I see," Kormak said.

"A mixture of sorcery and alchemy. A trick really. All the high powerful spells are beyond my strength now, otherwise I would not need your help."

Tarsus held up a hand and cocked his head to one side, listening. Kormak could not hear anything and he would have been willing to bet a gold solar to a copper farthing that his hearing was better than the wizards.

"They have begun," Tarsus said.

"I don't hear anything."

"There are other senses than the five most men rely on. I can sense the flows of power in this place. Someone is working a ritual."

"Why tonight?" Kormak asked.

Tarsus shrugged. "The moon is near full. The Lady's gaze always looks favourable on the working of magic. It is a propitious time for rituals. And now they have your blade with which to compel the demon."

"There's another reason, isn't there?"

"I think Lord Tomas was nervous for all his talk. He needed your blade for reassurance and he needed a host for the Ghul. Events tonight conspired to force him into a decision."

"A host?"

"It's not easy to communicate with the bodiless. Better to have it embedded in a mortal form. Easier to slay it with your blade if things go badly. They did not want to use you because they are afraid of your order and because you might be able to resist the possession."

"Who are they going to use?"

"Lady Kathea."

"What?"

"It wasn't the way they originally planned it—they were going to use a servant—but Lord Tomas was quite hurt by her infidelity."

That made the nobleman seem almost human. Kormak did not know whether that made him better or worse.

"What will happen to her?"

"The demon will devour her soul and take possession of her physical shell. It will wear her body. It's not a bad plan actually. She is weaker than they are and even if the demon masters the body quickly it should not pose too great a physical threat."

"We must save her."

"Youthful chivalry is an appalling thing," said Tarsus. "It makes men stupid."

"You are not suggesting we should let her die, are you?"

"If the demon is embodied we can kill it."

"Is there no other way?"

"We can stop the ritual before it goes too far although we may already be too late for that."

"Anything else?"

"If you can keep them busy, I might be able to compel the Ghul back into the bottle by reversing the spell. It is by no means a certainty though."

"I'll take any chance I can get."

"Very well but if worst comes to worst and the demon becomes corporeal don't hesitate, strike it down with that sword of yours."

"First I will need to get my hands on it."

"There is that," said Tarsus. "Still I have every confidence in you."

Kormak was not sure he had every confidence in himself. He was still recovering from his ordeal in the storm. He was not at his fighting peak. He hoped there were not any guards between them and the vault.

They pressed on along the corridor. Kormak felt the oppressive weight of the old buildings above him. He realised that this ancient passageway went a long way down below the earth. The stonework supporting the ceilings looked strong but it did not look modern. The flagstones beneath their feet had been worn away by the passage of countless feet.

"What was this place?"

"It was a chapel to the Old Gods, I suspect," Tarsus said. "Certainly the altar below bears their markings."

"That is never a good sign," said Kormak.

"Not all those who were worshipped before the coming of the Holy Sun were evil."

"It seems like a singularly appropriate place for a ritual to free a Ghul," said Kormak. He was starting to feel tense. He could sense the presence of swirling currents of magical energy in the air. He realised that Tarsus must be much more sensitive to these things than he was.

The old wizard paused. He was wheezing and his breath was coming out in clouds. It was getting colder. Kormak wondered whether it was just the chill of being underground or whether this was some sort of byproduct of the ritual.

"Are you all right?" he asked.

"No," the wizard said. "I have not been all right for a very long time but I can go on now." Kormak realised how desperate the venture was now. It was just him and this old sick man, trying to prevent the freeing of an ancient evil that it had taken the mightiest sorcerer who had ever lived to bind.

From down below, he could hear chanting. He thought he recognised the voices, muffled as they were. They belonged to Tomas and someone else: Wesley. "Why not just unstopper the flask?" Kormak asked.

"There are seals on it that must be removed and spells that must be in place to control the Ghul when it emerges, or at least constrain its freedom of action. They must bind it with a pentagram if they are to force it to do their bidding. They are rightly afraid of what may happen if it breaks free."

"And you are not?"

"I am terrified. It is all very well telling yourself that you do not care whether you live or die, but I find that when it comes to it I would rather go on living."

"Most people are like that."

"But you are not?"

"I long ago learned how to control my fear."

"The famous discipline of the Order of the Dawn. Alas it is too late for me to learn it now."

"You are doing pretty well. Wait here, I shall get a bit closer and find out what is going on." Tarsus sat down on the stair gratefully. Kormak hoped that Tomas and his companions did not hear the old man coughing.

He trod as lightly as he could down the stairs. The chanting became louder as he closed the distance. He found himself standing in the shadows of an archway looking into a large vault. Around the walls were various statues of animal-headed gods. In the centre was an altar, large enough for a human sacrifice.

Lady Kathea was on it, bound by chains of ancient black iron. Around the altar a pentacle had been laid out with salt. At the centre stood the ancient amphora. Lord Tomas read from an old scroll, intoning words in the Old Tongue that made Kormak's flesh creep. He wore the Elder Signs that had belonged to Kormak as well as some of his own.

Nearby stood Wesley. He had Kormak's blade in his hands. It was unsheathed. The disrespect filled Kormak with anger. Such a weapon was never supposed to be unsheathed unless you intended to kill. It was one of the oldest and strongest teachings of his order.

The man had no right to hold that weapon. He had not undergone the sacred cleansing or performed any of the rites of initiation. He had not been selected and judged worthy to bear the blade by another Guardian. It was a sort of sacrilege and Kormak, despite all his acquired cynicism, found he still had enough faith in what he did to feel outrage.

Not that it would do him much good while Wesley held the blade. Dwarf-forged steel was far sharper and stronger than any normal metal, lighter too, and there were runes worked into the blade to help it strike true. Those would work for anyone who bore it. Kormak could not help but notice that the runes on the naked blade were glowing. They were affected by the eddy currents of magic from the ritual.

Wesley advanced to where Kathea lay. She looked up, eyes wide with terror. She clearly understood all too well what her fate was intended to be. It was perfectly possible her husband had explained it to her in his calm, mad way. Wesley placed the flask upon the altar near her. It seemed to be shimmering now. Perhaps it was a trick of the torchlight but Kormak doubted it. It seemed that the spells were having some effect on the ancient binding. Or perhaps it was something else. Kormak did not know. He was not a sorcerer. His training had been in how to protect himself from evil magic when that was possible.

The knight held Kormak's blade at the ready. It was only then that Kormak realised what was intended and that he was too late to prevent the Ghul being freed. He raced forward to make the attempt anyway.

The knight took the dwarf-forged blade and brought its edge down on the seal of the flask severing it. Tomas smiled as a shimmering, shadowy, ectoplasmic form emerged from the mouth.

There would be no forcing the Ghul back into the jar now, Kormak realised. It was broken. They intended to bind the demon or kill it using his blade.

Kormak jumped over the salt lines of the pentacle being careful not to disturb the physical outline, knowing he was most likely disturbing the magical one. He landed close to the altar. Wesley saw him and strode to meet him. His strike was lightning fast. Kormak raised his blade to parry. The dwarf-forged sword notched its edge. Wesley pressed on with his attack and Kormak found himself on the defensive. Wesley was an excellent swordsman and in the peak of physical condition. Kormak was still weakened by his ordeal in the blizzard and the subsequent fever. Wesley was on him, cat-quick. Their swift footwork disturbed the salt, turning straight lines into scattered randomness.

Kormak parried again and again, too slow to find an opening in his opponent's guard.

"No, you idiots! You have ruined everything," Lord Tomas shouted. Over Wesley's shoulder, Kormak could see the ectoplasmic form was starting to take on a roughly humanoid shape.

Wesley grinned at him. White teeth showed like those of a skull. His eyes were dark and hooded and there was no mercy in them. "I had heard Guardian's were better swordsmen than this. It seems you are over-rated."

Kormak breathed deeply and sought ritual calmness. His movements began to flow better; he backed away and for a moment he and the knight traded blows, swords flickering too fast between them for the untrained eye to follow. Every blow left Kormak's blade more dented and notched and he feared it was only a matter of time before it broke, leaving him with only a shard in the haft. He began to appreciate exactly how much of an advantage the dwarf-forged blade had given him in his own duels.

Behind Wesley, the Ghul was beginning to flow towards Lord Tomas. The noble held up his hands in a warding gesture. The misty humanoid shape descended upon him, swirling like mist and the two came into contact. Lord Tomas screamed in a mixture of terror and rage. The Ghul recoiled, swirling away from the Elder Signs Tomas wore. Kormak realised there was another terrible danger here. Without his amulets he would be vulnerable to possession by the Ghul himself if it came for him. He began to move away from the altar. Taking his retreat for fear of the fight, Wesley grinned and closed in. His attacks became ever stronger as his confidence increased. Kormak made his own responses a little slower, as if he was weakening. It was not hard to simulate this, since he was.

The Ghul swirled over to the altar now and hovered over Lady Kathea. She looked up at it with wide, fear-filled eyes. Her mouth was tightly closed as if she was fighting to restrain her screams. The Ghul began to descend on her and paused. Doubtless it perceived that she was chained and this would place it at a terrible disadvantage if it took over her body. It clearly decided against making the attempt and moved away, flowing and wriggling through the air like an insubstantial, ghostly serpent.

Kormak snapped his head to one side as Wesley's blade cut his cheek, drawing blood. It stung. He realised that the lapse in concentration had almost cost him his life. Nonetheless, it was hard to give the fight his full attention when an even graver danger was closing in. He stepped closer to the knight and they were body to body, face to face. In their present condition, the knight was stronger. Kormak did not care. Seeing the sneer on Wesley's face, he brought his own head snapping forward, head-butting the man in the nose. Something splintered, blood flowed. Kormak struck with his sword but his timing was off. Wesley got his own weapon in the way but was knocked off balance and fell backward, stumbling. The dwarf-forged blade fell from his hand and went skittering across the floor, disturbing the salt lines even more.

The Ghul swirled ever closer. Wesley did not see it. Kormak did. He dived for his blade, reaching out to grasp it and then rolled to his feet. At once he felt better, more confident, the master of the situation. His sword was in his hand again. He felt whole.

The Ghul descended on Wesley. The knight's eyes widened and he screamed. His outline blazed and it looked for a moment like he had caught fire. Then the glow concentrated itself in his eyes, and Kormak saw something alien and wicked staring out of them. An odd burbling laugh emerged from the possessed man's mouth.

"Free! Razhak is free! At last!" He spoke the words in the Old Tongue.

Kormak stepped forward determined to run the demon through with his sword. The glow was already fading in its eyes and it looked completely human now. Its eyes widened as it saw what Kormak carried and recognised its fatal potential. It realised its hands were empty and it turned to run.

Kormak felt his limbs begin to slow. Suddenly he felt feverish. No, he thought this was not the time for his illness to recur. Then he realised it had not. Lord Tomas was chanting a spell, and it was taking its toll on Kormak.

Kormak's gaze flickered towards the Ghul. Tarsus was trying to block Wesley's escape, but the possessed knight simply punched him in the face with one gauntleted fist. The old wizard's head snapped back and he fell. Kormak felt a wave of dizziness overcome him and realised that Lord Tomas had somehow increased the power of his spell. Kormak turned to face him, barely able to stand. The noble continued to chant. Kormak could barely manage to remain on his feet.

Gathering his willpower he reeled towards Tomas, so dizzy he was certain he was not going to be able to make it. All he was doing was putting himself within striking distance. There was nothing else he could think to do.

His feet felt like lead. The contents of his stomach threatened to pour from his throat. The whole room seemed to turn on its axis. Lord Tomas smiled in triumph. Behind him Lady Kathea rose from the altar. She lifted the heavy weight of chains and bunched them in her hands and then swung them with all her strength at the back of her husband's head. Tomas fell as if pole-axed. Kormak lunged forward with his blade and took him through the chest. Tomas turned and looked at him, surprise and shock in his eyes. "That was not very sporting," he said. "I expected better of you, Guardian."

Kormak pulled his blade free then turned and tried to stagger after the fleeing Wesley, passing the slumped form of Tarsus on the stairs. He was panting when he reached the top. He could see that the main gate was open and the tracks of a horse led from it. Wesley or the thing that possessed him had fled into the night. Kormak needed to find his horse and pursue.

He noticed men at arms racing towards him. Some of them held swords, some of them held crossbows. A few of them were already moving to shut the gate. The rest of them surrounded him.

"You must let me go," Kormak said. "The demon is free."

"You are going to a cell," said the guard. "Till we get to the bottom of this."

Kormak considered jumping them, but they were too well-armed. All it would take was a single crossbow bolt and there would be no one to hunt down the demon.

"You are making a mistake," Kormak said.

"We'll see about that," said the guard.

Lady Kathea entered the cell, flanked by men at arms. She looked Kormak up and down and said, "I must apologise for the misunderstanding, Sir Guardian. I have explained what happened to the guards. They now know that Sir Wesley went mad and killed Lord Tomas. They know he stole our master's treasures."

Kormak shrugged. He knew she was telling him this so he did not contradict her story. He was glad she was on his side but it had taken her time to sort things out and now the Ghul had a full day's lead. It would take Kormak some time to overhaul it and by that time it might have found a new victim, making the hunt far more difficult.

"Where is the wizard, Tarsus?" Kormak asked.

"He is in a bad way," Kathea said. "He was extremely ill and he hit his head badly when Sir Wesley struck him. I doubt he has long to live. He was a very frail old man."

"Give him my best wishes," Kormak said. "I need my horse and my sword and my Elder Signs."

"You are going after Sir Wesley?" Lady Kathea asked.

"I don't have much choice," said Kormak so softly only she could hear. "The Ghul is free and someone needs to stop it."

"Does it have to be you?" she asked. "I am mistress here now and I could find a place for you in my retinue."

"You already know the answer to that," said Kormak. "Anyway, you already got what you really wanted."

"What was that?"

"Revenge on your husband. His estate for yourself."

"I find I could dislike you, Sir Kormak."

"Many people do," he said.

The snow had stopped. Tracks led away east towards the Mountains of Darkness. Kormak adjusted his scabbard and drew his cloak tight then urged his horse onwards. Behind him, on the battlements surrounding the manor, Lady Kathea waved.

Kormak did not wave back. He kneed his horse forwards, towards the distant peaks.

THE WOLVES OF WAR

THE WHITE EYE of the watching moon glared down on the burning village. Corpses sprawled everywhere. Most of the dead looked as if they had fled in panic and been overtaken by large beasts. Their flesh was ripped and their bones had been broken and gnawed for marrow. When he'd heard the sounds of violence and cries of pain Kormak had almost ridden on. After all, the civil strife tearing apart the Kingdom of Valkyria was not his fight, but the eerie howling told him there was work for him here.

Another strange echoing cry rang out through the cold night air. It sounded like the baying of a wolf but there was also something almost human in that call. It was answered from a different part of the village. Kormak reached for his sword but he did not draw it. He would only do that if he intended to kill.

His horse snorted skittishly although it had been trained to endure far worse than this. He got down from its back to inspect the dead.

He had been hoping to find a bed for the night in the local inn. The long chase after the Ghul Razhak through these mountains had left him badly in need of rest. Instead of sleep, he had found only horror and death. It must have come recently, for the bodies were still warm and the blood around some of them had not even started to congeal.

Something huge loped towards him out of the darkness. It had the shape of a man but it was bigger, perhaps half again as tall and perhaps three times as heavy. Greyish fur covered its body. Its head resembled a combination of a man and a wolf. Around its throat was a chain of nocturnium, one of the ancient night-metal alloys, forged into strange and terrible Elder Signs.

The monster opened its mouth and howled. Its long pink tongue lolled from its open maw. Its massive yellowish fangs glittered in the moonlight. Spittle drooled from its jaws and dripped onto the ground.

Hunger burned in its eyes as it moved ever closer. It came on with a terrible confidence, as if certain that it could not possibly be opposed by the man in front of it. It sprang, its leap carrying it far further than any human could jump. It stretched out its arms, long claws glittering in the moonlight, bright with the promise of death.

Kormak stepped to one side. His dwarf-forged blade leapt from its sheath, slashed outwards and parted the creature's head from its shoulders. Its skin sizzled where the sword edge bit. Even as he watched, the wolf-man changed back into a human being. Its corpse lay there in a pool of pink pus.

Another howl rang out, as if in answer to the dying wolf-man's cry, followed by a cry of pain.

Kormak moved through the streets of the burning village towards the sounds of screaming. He had heard that things were bad in the Mountains of Darkness and it seemed that he had not been misinformed. He passed a temple, a small shrine really, on fire in the middle of the village. The symbol of the Holy Sun was inscribed on the burning spire. He knew that these people were of the same faith that he himself followed.

He emerged into the middle of the temple square where another wolf-man confronted a villager armed only with a scythe. He was standing over the recumbent form of another human, trying to protect him. The wolf-man advanced with a lazy confidence that seemed entirely justified. The man slashed at it and his blade pierced the creature's flesh. The skin knitted behind the cut, there was no blood, and it was as if the creature had never taken a wound. Some magic protected it from the effects of normal weapons. Kormak began to understand how just two of these monsters had been able to slaughter the entire village.

Kormak shouted, trying to get the monster's attention. The peasant looked at him and in the moment when he was distracted, the wolf-man reached out and lazily tore his head off. It stood there, clutching the severed head, blood dripping over its talons. Its mouth lolled open and it seemed almost to be laughing. Kormak walked towards it, blade held at the ready. In the moonlight, the runes on the sword glowed slightly, telling Kormak of the presence of magic, even though he did not need told that at the moment.

The wolf-man seemed confused. Kormak guessed that it was not used to having its victims advance upon it, showing no fear. He also guessed that the creature sensed the power within his dwarf-forged weapon and was alarmed by it. Perhaps it smelled the blood of its companion on him.

Before Kormak could do anything, the wolf-man turned and fled, bounding away faster than a horse could run. It sprang over the wall of the village and raced off into the night. Kormak could hear its howling receding into the distance and knew that he could not overtake it.

He looked around him one more time and could see nothing but dead bodies and burning buildings. There was no sign of any further monsters so he strode over to where the headless villager lay. Beside him was a wounded man in the robes of a priest, a great gash torn in his flesh. Looking at his wound, Kormak knew the man did not have long to live. "What happened here?" he asked.

The priest looked up at him. "Massimo's Wolves came. They killed everyone."

"Massimo?" Kormak asked.

"Jaro's henchman. The wizard. Moondog rebels, the pair of them. Kill them, Champion of the Sun. Kill them all." He coughed blood and tried to make the sign of the Sun over his ripped chest. His eyes went wide and cold and Kormak realised that the last thing he had seen was the moon, an ill omen for a man of his faith.

Kormak picked his way through the ruins of the village, looking for survivors. There were none. The wolf-men had been thorough about their work. On his way back, he checked the body of the wolf-man he had killed. It still lay there, in a puddle of what looked like liquified flesh. The night-metal necklace glittered on its throat. Looking closely Kormak could see that it seemed to have fused into the flesh.

Kormak prised it free. It tingled in his hand as he touched it. He could feel the foulness in it, the taint of Shadow. It shattered when he struck it with his blade.

A wisp of ectoplasm drifted free and he ran his blade through it too, dissolving it and sending the bound spirit to its final death. Whoever this Massimo was, Kormak thought, he knew powerful dark magic.

He did not want to take his rest surrounded by the dead, and perhaps the wolf-man would return with companions.

In the distance Kormak could see smoke rising. There had been a lot of it since he had started riding through the Mountains of Darkness. Everywhere he looked there was burning and the signs of strife. It felt wrong. It was late autumn, not the time for local lordlings to be making war. He had seen more burned-out villages with the charred bodies of massacre victims strewn through them. He had seen farms and cottages burned to the ground. He had seen the flocks of sheep slain and left to rot.

He had been born in the mountains of Aquilea, a rough land, where clan feuds burned hot and long but he had never seen anything like this. Flocks were for rustling, not to kill and leave lying. This was more like the work of mad beasts than men. It was as if madness had struck right across the mountains.

He had seen their tracks, those of large, armed bands, leading away from the place where the massacres happened. Mingled with those of horses and men had been what looked like those of very large dogs. He guessed the wolf-men rode with the warriors.

Ahead of him he saw a body on the road. There was something about this that was at once repulsive and disturbing.

He reined his horse to halt and dismounted to inspect the corpse. He noticed the smell from many strides away, a peculiar mixture of rotting meat and something else, something suggestive of things long dead. He had a suspicion he knew what he would find even before he reached the body and he was not disappointed.

He knew the man, or he had known in him life. It was the robber-knight Wesley. His features seemed to have aged and at the same time putrefied. His body and his life had been consumed by the Ghul who had possessed him. It feasted on the life energy of its victims even as it took possession of their bodies.

The process was happening faster than it ought to according to the old records. Perhaps the Ghul had been weakened by millennia of imprisonment. Or perhaps some of Solareon's spells binding it were still in place. In any case, this might perhaps represent a strange stroke of luck. If the Ghul needed to shift bodies constantly it would be easier to identify as the bodies decomposed and it would find it more difficult to locate new victims who would be wary of its appearance.

It seemed like it had already found a new victim, one who had not been wary enough, or perhaps one who had simply been overpowered by the knight. It occurred to Kormak that he had no idea what the new victim looked like. There did not seem to be any witnesses. He studied the ground for clues and found a staff and a bundle lying nearby, the sort that a tinker or an itinerant labourer might have carried. Had these belonged to Razhak's last victim or was there no connection? In the absence of any further indicators, he would need to presume that there was a connection.

He looked around for tracks and found none. He had encountered no one on the road, so the Ghul had not doubled back. It was probably safe to assume that it was still fleeing before him, but for how long would that continue? If it reached a town it would have many more potential victims and many more ways to cover its tracks. Of course, there might be mages there who could help hunt it down. Kormak knew if the hunt took much longer he would need to seek the aid of a wizard himself. He could not simply rely on luck.

Part of him wondered why he was doing this at all. He could simply turn back and leave the Ghul to go on its way. No one would know but him. He could just turn his horse around and head west, back to Taurea and the home of his order. There was nothing to stop him. There were even those who would argue that it was his duty to do so, but he could not bring himself to believe that. The monster was free at least in part because he had failed. Lord Tomas and Wesley had taken his sword and his gear and used it in the ritual that had set Razhak free. It would not have happened if he had not been present and too weak to stop them.

Even as he pondered this he thought he heard movement in the undergrowth nearby. His hand went to the hilt of his sword. If Razhak was present he would need to defend himself. He walked closer to where the sound was coming from and he thought he heard sobbing. He kept one hand on the sword hilt and he pulled the bushes apart. Something looked up at him, large eyes staring fearfully out of a dirt-smudged face. It took Kormak a moment to realise it was a teenage girl.

She looked at Kormak. He inspected her for signs of possession.

"You just going to stare at me?" she asked. Kormak tilted his head to one side. She moved her hand. There was a knife in it. "If you come any closer I will stick you."

She glared. He studied the pupils of her eyes. They were wide but they looked normal. There was no glaze and she was not looking at him fixedly. Her mannerisms were normal although that might not mean anything. A Ghul like Razhak had centuries to learn how to counterfeit those.

"What's your name?" Kormak asked. He watched, listening closely for the slightest hesitation.

"Who's asking?"

"My name is Kormak. I am a Guardian of the Order of the Dawn."

"Yes and I am Our Lady of the Moon."

"I would not say that too loudly where the Old Ones might hear," Kormak said.

"It's daylight. They do not come out in the sunlight." She sounded normal but he had not really heard enough to judge. He needed to keep her talking. He needed to collect more information. Sometimes the only way to tell if someone was possessed was to look for small cues in their manner. He doubted that anyone who Razhak was within would rant and rave like a lunatic. The Ghul did not seem to be that sort of demon.

"Most of them can't. Some can cloak themselves with spells. Others can take possession of human or animal forms. Sometimes they have other gifts. They can hear or see things a long way off. Particularly concerning things that are of interest to them."

"You sound like a Guardian."

"How would you know? Have you ever met one?"

"You sound like what they are supposed to sound like."

"What is your name?"

"Are you on a quest?"

"I am hunting a monster. I am trying to decide whether you are what I am looking for."

She looked insulted and then a little frightened and she brought the knife between them. She held it edge on, more as a barrier than as if she knew how to use it. She would have had the point towards him if she did.

"And if you think I am the one you are looking for, you will kill me, won't you?"

He nodded.

"You'll try," she said.

"No. I will kill you," he said. "It is what I do. That tiny knife won't stop me. You can't even hold it properly."

His voice was flat and calm and that just made it more frightening. She flinched away from him.

"You really would, wouldn't you?"

"I really would."

"And you're the sort of cold bastard who would tell me that as well."

"I am trying to get a sense of who you are and whether you are possessed."

"Like by a demon?"

"Yes."

"It's not an accident you are on this road. You are looking for something that looked like a rotting corpse walking."

"I am."

"It looks like the nastiest beggar you ever saw, smelled worse, smelled so bad you knew it could not be anything good."

"You've seen it?"

"Why do you think I am hiding here?"

"I have no idea. I am trying to find out."

"So you can decide whether or not to kill me." He did not say anything, just watched her. He was ready for anything or he thought he was. He was not prepared when she laughed and said, "You're as bad as the Wolves."

"Who are they?"

"You've just ridden into these parts, haven't you?"

"Yes."

"They're who has been burning and raping and looting and killing. They're the worst of the worst, the remnants of Jaro's army and something even nastier."

"Who is Jaro?"

"Jaro was the Pretender. He raised his banner here in the mountains, declared himself king. A load of the local lads thought he'd make a good one so they signed on with him."

"The real king of Valkyria decided different."

"Who is to say who is the real king?"

"The one with the victorious army."

"You're not as dumb as you look, are you? Yeah—King Sturmbrand scattered Jaro's rebels at Hell Ford. They say he struck down the Pretender with his blade Lightning but the body was never found. Massimo, Jaro's pet wizard, retreated into the mountains to cook up some new devilry. The Wolves appeared soon after that."

"So you've got what's left of a rebel army riding around and plundering."

"That's how it started. Have you decided whether you are going to kill me or not?"

"Not yet. Keep talking."

"You could be one of them, you know. You've got the eyes."

"Have I?"

"Flat and cold and with a real distance in them. You've killed a lot of people, haven't you?"

"Yes."

"And you don't even have to think about it or look embarrassed or ashamed when you say it?"

"Should I?"

"You obviously don't think so. You're proud of it, aren't you?"

"No. It's my calling. You were telling me about the Wolves."

"They used to be called that because of the wolf's head on Jaro's banner. But since they started following his lieutenant, Massimo, the sorcerer, some of them have become real wolves. You heard of Massimo?"

"No."

"He's a bad one, has made pacts with the Shadow, so they say, and if you really are a Guardian you should take a look at him."

"I might."

"You would never get within a hundred feet of him. The Wolves would tear you apart."

"His pets are nasty?"

She laughed bitterly. "They're not pets. They are men. Or at least they once were men. He did something to them during the rebellion, changed them in some way. Now they are something different. At night, they can change into monsters. You know, I really am starting to believe you are a Guardian. A normal man would be back on his horse and riding for his life about now. You just stand there as if you've heard this sort of thing all before."

"I have."

"So are you going to do anything about it? Somebody ought to make Massimo and his bastard monsters pay for what they are doing."

"It sounds like it will take more than one lone Guardian to do that."

"I thought you lot were supposed to be heroes, sneer in the face of danger, defy demons, that sort of thing."

"I am sorry to disappoint. I already have one monster I am tracking. Are you going to tell me what you know about it?"

"So you are convinced that I am not it?"

"Maybe."

"Cagey bastard, aren't you?"

"It's how I have lived to my advanced age."

"It's a skill I wish you would teach me."

"What is your name, girl?"

"Petra."

"What are you doing on this road?"

"My brother and I were fleeing, trying to get away."

"From where?"

"Oakbridge. It was our village back along the road. The Wolves burned it."

"You fled?"

"We fled. We were the only ones left alive. Luck really. Our house was on the edge of the village furthest from where they broke in. Tam smelled the burning, woke me. We crept out and hid, dived into the millpond. That way the Wolves could not smell us."

"Clever."

"Tam was a good hunter. He knew about such things. He taught me what he could after our parents died."

"Where is he now?"

"You already know, don't you?"

"The demon took him, or it took his body."

"It was horrible. I could hear him screaming. He told me to run then he told me to come back. The voice did not sound like him at all."

"It wasn't. It was the thing that killed him."

"He's dead then."

"His body is walking the world. His soul is not in it though."

"Then I can't even give him a proper burning."

"You follow the Solar rites here?"

"Our village did. It's all mixed up here though in the mountains. Some are moondogs. There's old hatred here. Massimo is a moondog, so are his Wolves. You'd better hope they don't see you. You're sworn to the Sun, aren't you?"

"I was. A long time ago."

"You going to kill me or not?" Kormak looked at her. She was just a girl, with eyes that looked as if they were about to brim with tears, who had been hungry for too long. At least as far as he could tell.

"How did Razhak catch you?"

"Razhak? Is that the sort of demon you are chasing?"

"It's his name."

If she was curious as to how he knew that, she gave no sign. "He rode up, on a big horse. I thought there was something odd about him. It was the smell. We started to run but he rode Tam down. He just passed me by."

"I don't think Razhak would want a woman's body here. It would make him too vulnerable."

"You make it sound very cunning."

"A land torn by war. A woman on her own. Too much like a victim."

"He might use it as a trap."

"You do think like a hunter."

"I can help you hunt this bastard demon," she said. "It killed my brother."

"I am not sure I want any help."

"You going to do this all on your own?"

"I don't want to hunt a demon and look after you at the same time."

"You are the soul of chivalry, aren't you? A real knight."

"A real knight would beat you for showing such disrespect. They don't like uppity peasant girls."

"So I should be glad you're not? And I am not a peasant. I am a freeholder."

"You got any place to go, or were you and your brother just fleeing?"

"My father's sister has a place down in Steelriver. She would take us in. Or she'll take me in now."

"How far is Steelriver?"

"It's the main town about five leagues ahead. It's mostly a Sunlander place and it's too big for the Wolves to attack, yet. All the Sunlanders are heading that way. What? What did I say? You look as if you swallowed a lemon."

Kormak thought about what she had said. He suddenly saw a pattern to all the burnings. "It's a cattle drive," he said. "They are burning you out and driving you all to one place."

She looked at him. Her mouth opened as if she was about to contradict him but then it closed again. "You know, you might be right."

"There's been a lot of feuding between the Sunlanders and the moondogs hasn't there?"

"Always has been since Kyril the Conqueror claimed these lands in the name of the Holy Sun. The moondogs don't like that one little bit."

Kormak nodded. He could tell the girl was talking about humans when she mentioned moondogs. Further west that particular name was reserved for the Old Ones themselves not those who worshipped them. Here the words had the sound of a most bitter insult.

"You think they are going to get everyone in one place and then burn it?"

"It's an old trick in siege warfare. Force your enemy to open the gates to refugees from their own side. If they open the gates, it's more mouths to feed. If they turn them away, it demoralises."

"Lord Martin would not turn any one of the True Faith away. The city council might. They are a bunch of money grubbing bastards by all accounts."

"You always use such language?"

"Who are you, my father?"

"Where is he?"

"Dead, like my mother. Red plague took them."

Kormak could tell by the set of her mouth that she was not going to say anything more on that subject.

"You can walk with me to Steelriver. Razhak is most likely going that way anyway."

And that would not be good, Kormak thought. There would be many new bodies there, and in a big town he could hide all too well.

"You not going to ask me to ride with you?"

"My horse does not need the extra weight and I don't need anyone behind me who is so ready with a knife."

They had been on the road for hours and Kormak was tired of fending off the girl's endless questions. He just stared at their surroundings and let her chatter flow over him. She did not seem to care so long as he grunted occasionally as if he were listening.

It was getting dark. The mountains which mere hours before had been vast and clear, dappled with woods, bright with snow on the peaks, were becoming mere gigantic shadows that loomed menacingly all around. Clouds hid the face of Our Lady of the Moon. It did not look like they would make the town this evening so it was time to make camp.

Kormak swung his steed off the road when he found a convenient hollow. It was cold, with the chill of oncoming winter. He began to gather sticks for a fire. Petra began to help. He noticed that she had a leather strap in her hand now with a stone in it and he watched her warily. Many a warrior had been killed with a sling. It made him reluctant to remove his helmet. He had known some men who would have mocked him for that but he was still alive and they were long in their graves.

"You any good with that?" he asked.

She nodded and began to whirl the sling. He kept his eye on her, ready to throw himself to one side if she looked like she was bringing it to bear on him. The stone whizzed away and brought down a squirrel in a nearby tree. It was an excellent shot in the bad light.

"Impressive," Kormak said.

"Dinner," she said. She nodded at the sword. "You any good with that thing?"

"I don't intend to bring down any squirrels with it."

"It was not squirrels I was thinking of," she said. She nodded towards the mountain slope. There was something moving amid the undergrowth there. It might have been a wolf or a bear. Kormak returned to getting the fire lit. It might prove useful in keeping beasts at bay as well as keeping them warm. Petra moved closer. She set the squirrel down and began to clean and skin it. She carefully placed the pelt aside. He guessed she might be able to sell it or the tail. Or maybe she wanted to use it herself.

"You don't seem too worried," she said. He could tell whatever was out there was on her mind.

"If we have to fight, we have to fight," he said. "I am not worried. I have an expert slinger on my side."

"It was a lucky shot," she said. "And I can't bring down a bear."

"It seems to be heading away anyway."

"It might come back."

"Worry about it when it happens."

"Can you really do that? Push everything out of your mind."

"No," said Kormak. "But I can try."

She put the squirrel on the end of a twig and began to roast it over the fire. "You want some?" she asked.

"I have waybread."

"You going to offer me some?"

"I thought your offer of roast squirrel was not entirely altruistic." He offered her some of the waybread anyway and shook his head as she pushed the squirrel forward. She took the waybread.

"You speak like the preachers who used to come round the villages."

"I was educated in a monastery."

"Mount Aethelas?"

"Yes."

"You're not a Sunlander. Why did they take you in?"

"The Holy Sun accepts all those who accept him."

"And you accepted him?"

"The Aquileans worshipped the Sun before the Solari came from over the World Ocean."

"You did not answer my question."

"That might give you a clue that I am not going to."

"Keep your blade handy. The Wolves roam the night."

"I think we'll notice if a band of riders comes thundering out of the dark."

"Sometimes the wolf-men hunt on their own."

"You're not frightened, are you?"

"Why should I be? I have a Guardian here to protect me."

"Who is going to protect me?"

"You are not quite as reassuring as the stories say you should be."

"Worry about the wolf-man when the wolf-man comes. Or leave it to me to worry about. Get some sleep."

She seemed to already have taken him at his word. A sound of snoring emerged from the other side of the fire. Kormak made sure his blade was close at hand, wrapped himself in his cloak and stared at the sky. There was a moisture in the air, a dampness that reminded him of the mountains of his homeland. It made him feel almost nostalgic. He avoided looking at the fire. He did not want to ruin his night vision.

The whinnying of the horse woke Kormak. His steed was a warhorse, trained to remain calm in the face of battle, fire and monsters. It was nervous now though and that in turn made him nervous. He rose to his feet, reaching for his blade. The girl was already up with her knife out.

"Planning on slitting my throat in the dark, were you?" Kormak asked.

"Your horse woke me. There's something out there. Maybe the bear has come back."

"Maybe," Kormak said. He sniffed the air. There was an odd scent to it, of fur and something else. It was not the rotten smell he would have associated with Razhak's walking corpse.

Something big emerged from the shadows. Kormak turned to face it. He did not draw his sword despite feeling an almost overpowering urge to do so. The creature was bigger than he was and covered in fur but it was not a bear. It walked upright like a man and its body resembled that of a man save for being broader and more stooped. The arms were longer and the hands ended in claws. It had a wolf's head although the brow was higher and the eyes wider, and there was an odd intelligence in them. Around its neck was a choker of night-metal like the other wolf-men had worn.

"It's one of Massimo's Wolves," said Petra.

"I worked that out all by myself," Kormak said, not taking his eyes from the creature.

"Are you going to kill it?"

"Not unless it attacks us," said Kormak loud enough so the wolf-man could hear what he was saying. Looking at those huge pointed ears he suspected it would have been able to do that even if he whispered. It opened its muzzle and let its tongue loll out, almost as if it was laughing. Kormak took a slow step closer. He wanted it to understand he was not afraid of it either. It looked at him with those fierce, red, miserable eyes. Kormak could see its muscles tense, as if it were about to spring.

"I would not do that if I were you," he said. "Not unless I wanted to die."

That seemed to be all the trigger it took. The wolf-man sprang, an avalanche of fur and muscle and rage slammed into Kormak. Its weight knocked him over but already it was ceasing to struggle.

"I don't believe it," said Petra. "You drew your sword and put it through the wolf-man's chest in a heartbeat."

Kormak pushed the heavy corpse off him. "Yes," he said sourly.

Kormak looked down at the wolf-man. It was already beginning to change. A pinkish-grey pus was leaking from its flesh as it lost mass and began to revert to something more human. In a few heartbeats a tall man clad in what looked like rags was lying there. He was still alive despite the fact that Kormak's sword was embedded in his abdomen. Kormak had no intention of taking it out until he was certain the man was dead.

"Thank you," said the man. It was not exactly what Kormak had expected.

He hunkered down beside the man. "Why?"

"You have freed me, freed my soul. The demon in me is gone. It could not stand your sword. It burned."

"Massimo bound something into your body?"

The dying man nodded. "When Massimo brought Jaro back from the dead, he called for volunteers. He said Massimo would work magic, that would make us invincible, let us take back what was ours from the Sunlanders. He showed us what had been done to him, how the wolf spirit had been bound into him and made him mighty. I stepped forward."

"Kill the moondog bastard," said Petra. "He's slaughtered hundreds."

"I want to hear what he has to say."

The man's lips quirked in a sour smile. "She's right. I did. Men, women, children. It was not what I expected. Not what I was told. He put a demon in me, Massimo did. At first I thought I could control it, use its power but over the months it grew stronger. It fed on the rage and hate and pain. In the end it controlled me. It made me want to kill everything within reach . . ."

"Typical moondog bastard, always giving excuses when they are caught, when it doesn't matter. Tell the folks you killed you're sorry!"

"I am not sorry I killed most of them," the wolf-man said. "You came here and stole our land and you raised your false god. You persecuted those who followed the Old Ways and you were always so righteous about it. We showed you that Our Lady still has power."

Petra had drawn her knife. Kormak gestured for her to stand back. He did not want this man's throat cut, not yet anyway. "Massimo did this to you."

"Yes."

"Why did you come here? Why did you attack us? Did you just find our trail, catch our scent?"

"I was sent to find you. Many of the Wolves were. You are a champion of the Sun and you are pursuing Massimo's new friend. There will be others after you now. I was just the first to catch your trail."

"New friend?"

"Something strange. It rode up yesterday and chatted with Massimo for hours. It smelled of death and old magic. When he was finished, the sorcerer gave us our orders."

Kormak looked up at the sky. The clouds had parted. The waning moon blinked mockingly through the gap. "Where can I find Massimo?"

"The Devil's Peak," said the wolf-man.

"That's where his tower is," said Petra. "No one goes there."

"You can show me to this place?" he asked her. She looked at him for a long time, swallowed and nodded.

"I could but I won't. I am not mad. No one comes back from Devil's Peak."

"Razhak is there. He killed your brother. You said you wanted to revenge. You said you wanted Massimo dead."

"And you will kill him?"

"If I have to and I suspect I might."

"You don't lack confidence do you, big man?"

"I do what I have to, like everybody else. Massimo wants me dead. His Wolves want me dead. Razhak is with him. Under the circumstances, someone is going to die and it's not going to be me."

"If you go to the tower you will die, Guardian," said the wolf-man. "What's left of Jaro's army is camped in the valley and the Wolves guard Massimo. Not even your blade can kill all of them."

"There's more than one way to skin a wolf," Kormak said. "I don't plan on hacking my way in."

"I said you were not entirely stupid," said Petra. Her voice sounded so shaky Kormak knew she was still considering helping him. "You really mean to kill Massimo?"

"If I can."

"If you do there will be no more Wolves."

"Not unless Massimo's apprentices have been taught his secrets."

"Massimo has no apprentices," said the wolf-man. "He guards his secrets from all."

"Why is he helping Razhak?"

"I think Razhak has promised Massimo the secret of immortality. Does he really have it?"

"Only the Old Ones know that," said Kormak. "And he is not a true Old One."

The wolf looked curious. "I am sorry I don't have the time to find out what you mean." Blood was leaking from the corners of his mouth and from his nostrils now. His breathing was a hoarse rattle. There was a bubbling sound from inside his chest.

"You should just leave the bastard to be eaten by scavengers," Petra said as she placed another rough stone on top of the shallow grave. "There's no need to build the monster a monument."

"He died as a man and he repented," Kormak said.

"And you believed him?"

"I've seen others repent their wickedness. There's hope for us all."

"You seem to really need to believe that." She grunted as she lifted another heavy stone. Kormak looked at her and watched until she had lowered it into place.

"You always watch, don't you? You looked at me as if you were expecting me to try and brain you with that rock."

"I am not entirely certain you were not considering it."

"If you are going to kill Massimo I want you to live. He's the bastard who deserves to die. That wolf would have eaten me as it raped me if you had not killed it. I owe you for that."

"I can't kill Massimo if I can't find him."

"All right, I'll show you the way to Devil's Peak."

"Thank you." She laughed.

"What's funny?"

"You. I offer to show you the way to certain death and you thank me. You're a strange man, Guardian."

"I live in a strange world."

"We all do."

"I've seen more of it than most folk." Kormak placed another rock on the cairn and watched her as she took her turn. This time she met his gaze and just kept laughing.

They left the main road and started up a mountain track. This was clearly a path and a well-used one but it was not anything like a highway.

"Used to be drovers and rustlers used these tracks," Petra said. "The high valleys are full of treacherous, thieving moondogs."

"So you've said," Kormak said. "Many times."

"If I am boring you, just say so," said the girl.

"I have said so."

"I didn't say I would pay any attention," she said.

"You talk because you're scared, I understand that." She looked insulted and she shut up for a few minutes as he suspected she would. He was enjoying the silence when she said. "You think you're very clever, don't you?"

"Do I?"

"You think you can make me shut up by implying I am a coward if I talk."

"I can see you are too cunning for me."

"No. I am not. You were right. I am scared. I've been scared for a very long time. Since the war started. Since before the war started, when you could see it coming and the preachers were whipping everybody up to hate and the moondogs were spitting on our shadows and throats were being slit in the night. I was scared when the traders started bringing stories of battles and even when the King's armies won. We were scared they would increase out taxes, and then we learned Jaro wasn't dead and the Wolves were still out there. It was almost a relief when Oakbridge was attacked. It was like the worst had come and there was nothing more to worry about, but there was, wasn't there? There always is. There always will be."

She looked like a pale and frightened child now, like she always had been although he had been too annoyed and distracted to see it. He did not know what to say, so he kept quiet. He did not look at her. He heard soft noises that sounded like sobbing. They went on for a long time and then she blew her nose. That went on for a long time too.

Eventually she said, "How do you get to be a Guardian?"

"You thinking of becoming one?"

"I might if I could."

There was no way she could become one. She was too old. She was not a Sunlander. He shook his head as he raised that objection. He was not a Sunlander either but then the order had special reasons for making him one of their own. "You must be presented at Mount Aethelas," he said. "And you must swear an oath by the Holy Sun."

"That's all?"

"There's the learning and the training, that takes some time."

"They teach you how to use the sword?"

"Yes. And to read and to write."

"That sounds boring."

"How else will you be able to read your instructions from the Grand Master or find out what you need to know about the Old Ones in the lorebooks."

"I thought you memorised all that, the way bards learn their chants."

"You memorise a lot but you can't learn everything. There's always something more to find out."

"All right, I'll give you that it's useful but it's still dull."

"I thought so when they first started teaching me but I soon got interested."

"You have a priestly look about you so I am not surprised."

"Most people find me menacing."

"You'd like to think that, wouldn't you?"

"In my experience it's true."

"I thought that when I first saw you. After I've talked to you, I am not sure. You do not seem like a mad-dog killer to me. If you had passed through our village dressed like a normal man I would never have guessed what you were."

"You're not exactly an expert on the subject."

"You're the one who asked for my help."

"I have been reduced to such desperate straits. It is sad."

"You killed that wolf-man back there, and you did not even look as if you were trying."

"People who are good at things make them look easy, even if they are difficult."

"Were you scared?"

"I did not have time to find out."

"What?"

"It was all over so quickly."

"Still, you must have worked out what to do; you must have thought about it."

"No. It happened too fast for that. That's why you train, so your body knows what to do automatically. You stop to think when you are fighting something like a wolf-man and you are dead."

"I'll take your word for it." She continued to look at him as if interested in learning some secrets he knew. Kormak wanted to tell her that there were no secrets, only hard work and luck and ruthless determination. He was not sure what good it would have done though so he kept quiet.

It was cold in the mountains but still warmer than Kormak would have expected for the time of year. Aquilea was a lot further coldward though so that might account for it. They said heat leeched away over the snowy edge of the world, the closer you got to it. It was certainly true it became warmer the further south you got.

The trees still had some of their leaves here and a riot of coloured flowers was still in bloom on thorny bushes. Their scents fought for attention in his nostrils. High overhead an eagle soared on the wind. Kormak was very aware of its presence and of the massive bulk of the mountains looming over him. He felt like an insect crawling over their sides and that got him to thinking.

"You are frowning. Straining to think, are you?" Petra said. He looked at her and smiled. They had developed the odd companionship of the road, the intimacy of strangers who would most likely never see each other again after the next few days. He had felt this way many times before. He could be open in such circumstances in a way he could not be with the closest brethren of his order.

"I was thinking about whether any of this is worth it."

"You picked a bad time to have doubts."

"I've always had them. Our lives are so short. We will pass in an eyeblink of the gods. The mountains will still be here. They've seen a hundred generations come and go. They'll see a hundred more."

She looked a little confused. "I have sometimes thought something similar myself."

"Razhak has been here for millennia. The Old Ones have been here even longer. I have set myself to hunt things as old as mountains and I do so to stop them preying on people who will die anyway, in heartbeats as those demons measure time."

"Why do it then? No one is forcing you to. You could just turn your horse around and ride away."

"You're not asking me anything I haven't asked myself."

"You ever give yourself any answers?"

"I swore an oath. I keep it."

"That's no answer at all."

"It is for me."

"It's not the whole truth though, is it?" It was a surprisingly sharp observation for one so young.

"The truth is that I love doing this. I love the hunt. I love the excitement of the battle. It's when I feel most alive."

"You could soon get very dead."

"And that's the point. Sometimes I think that is an unworthy reason to do what I do but it keeps me at the task."

"Maybe for you. I plan on living as long as I can and dying peacefully in my sleep surrounded by my grandchildren."

"I am surprised you have thought that far ahead."

"I've had some occasion to brood on these things recently. Tell me, do you hate him? Razhak, I mean? Or any of the Old Ones."

"I don't know Razhak. I know what he has done and what he will do if he is not stopped and that is enough for me."

"What about the Old Ones?"

"One in particular but it's an old hate and I try not to let it bother me."

"Why you hate the one you do?" Kormak considered his answer, wondering whether he should give one, and then decided that under the circumstances it did not matter at all.

"Because I am afraid of him and because he killed my family when I was a boy. He killed everyone I knew."

"I can understand why you feel that way then. You see that all the time up here. With the feuds. One killing leads to another. The moondogs kill us. We kill them. I was kind of hoping you would say there is no one you hate or fear."

"The two things go together along with a lot of other ugly emotions."

"You do sound like a priest sometimes, you know."

"I know."

"How are you going to kill Massimo?"

"However I can."

"That does not sound like a plan."

"How can I have a plan when I have no idea what I will encounter? I will sneak into the tower one way or another. I will find Massimo and Razhak then I will see what happens."

"You have a lot of confidence in your own ability, don't you?" She sounded envious.

"I've done this sort of thing before."

"And that's the secret, isn't it? To confidence, I mean. How do you do it the first time though?"

"You fumble your way through and you do your best to appear to know what you are doing."

"Is that what you did?"

"For the most part. I was also trained to do this. It helps. A lot."

"An order of monks who are trained to kill. It sounds more exciting than praying for the souls of the dead."

"I won't argue about that."

"But you could?"

He shrugged. Somewhere in the distance a howl rang out. It was eerily loud. It sounded like a wolf but it was not. There was something oddly human about its tones. Petra had frozen on the spot. Her face was pale and devoid of colour. Her knife was in her hands but she looked as if she wanted to dive into the nearest bush.

"It seems like Massimo's pets are getting ready to hunt," she said. Her voice sounded shaky, as if she was having some difficulty forcing the words out. She swallowed and waited for him to say something. He just listened.

"They are still a long way off. The sound carries a fair distance in these valleys."

"They are going to be looking for us soon."

"They are going to be looking for me. You can still run." She looked embarrassed.

"I don't want to be on my own in these mountains with the Wolves running free."

"We're heading towards an army."

"I can be as sneaky as you. I have hunted these hills since I was a little girl. And I want to be there when you kill Razhak. I want to see him pay for what he did to Tam."

"I am not sure that is a good idea."

"You think I am not up for it?"

"I've seen people who have had to deal with possessed relatives before. It's not pleasant. They sometimes forget what has happened and demons can be very persuasive."

"It won't happen to me."

"I wish I was as certain of anything, as you are of everything."

"You are getting old, Guardian."

"I know it." They moved on.

Below them the valley was visible in the early evening gloom. Smoke rose from campfires around which sat a number of men. A tower loomed on the opposite ridge overlooking the other side of the valley. A silvery dome topped the roof. It has the ancient look of most lunar fortifications in the area. The moondogs had been in this land a long time before the Sun worshippers came. It had been theirs once, just as the dying wolf-man had claimed.

The tower's age in no way detracted from its aura of strength. The position was very defensible, the only approach up the line of the ridge, a narrow road along which not many troops could advance at a time. Anyone coming up the road would be visible to defenders from a long way off. Anyone standing on the battlements would have a clear view of the surrounding land.

Kormak was glad that Petra had the native wit not to stand. He had left his horse back down the path a ways, and crawled forward to take a look. He did not want to be silhouetted against the brow of the ridge if anyone glanced in their direction.

"There are several hundred men down there, and most likely Wolves in the tower. They are not all out hunting us," Petra said. "Massimo must want to keep a guard close to him."

"Maybe he does not trust Razhak," Kormak said. "I can't say I would blame him."

"You think he took possession of one of the Wolves?"

"It would not do him much good."

"How so?"

"The wolf-man is already possessed. It has a spirit of Shadow bound within its form. It would fight possession by Razhak and even if he snatched the body, he would have none of its powers. They would go with the Shadow Spirit."

"He might have powers of his own."

"He most certainly does. He is a life drinker."

"And that does not scare you?"

"My amulets will protect me."

"I wish I had one."

"I need all the ones I have."

"I wasn't asking. I was just saying." She was very touchy and, of course, she had been asking. As they watched the gate of the tower opened and a pack of monstrous shapes emerged howling. They raced down the path and joined a group of riders. All of them departed from the valley by the entrance on the opposite side.

"It looks like the Wolves of War ride tonight," Petra said. "Another village will burn somewhere."

"At least they are not coming this way," Kormak said. "And they won't be in the tower when we come calling."

"How are you going to do this?"

"Leave the horse hobbled here and head down into the valley after dark. If it looks like we can, we'll just head up the ridge road. If not, we climb the cliffside."

"You sure you can do that in all that armour and stuff?"

"I was born in Aquilea. I learned to climb before I could walk."

"You're exaggerating, aren't you?"

"Only a bit."

"Well if you can climb it so can I." He looked at her. She seemed small and frightened but she had pasted a look of determination on her face.

"You sure you can do this?"

"If I am not quieter than you I'll pay you a silver piece."

"If you're not quieter than me, we both may be dead."

"Then at least I won't owe you my last farthing."

"It might be better if you stayed here."

"You don't get it, do you? There's nothing left for me. My brother is dead and possessed by a demon, my village is burned; there's nowhere to go. I have nothing to lose and I have a chance to pay that bastard Massimo back."

"What about your aunt?"

"I made her up." He looked at her for a long time. He had not believed she could surprise him, but she had.

"Well, let's find out if you made up the part about being stealthy as well."

They moved quietly down the narrow path into the valley. It twisted down the hillside. Kormak realised that Petra was as good a huntress as she had claimed. The girl made no more noise than he did. She had her sling in her hands and her knife at the ready and for once she had stopped talking. He found that he missed her chatter now that it had ceased.

They reached the valley floor and he saw that there were still a number of camps scattered through the valley. Why were the forces split, he wondered? His best guess was that the different camps were the followers of different captains or nobles.

Slowly and carefully they moved forward. It was painstaking and tiring work. He could see that there were pickets set, and guards moving around. Did the moondogs really expect to be attacked here or was it that they did not trust each other or Massimo's pets? Possibly it was all three reasons. It made life more difficult for him because even in the gloom, runners moved from camp to camp and men drifted backwards and forward between the fires, most likely visiting acquaintances and friends.

He gestured for Petra to freeze as he heard boots come clumping out of the dark. He held his blade ready to draw if they were noticed. Under the circumstances it would probably be better to use his hands. The sounds of combat would simply draw attention to them. They needed to pass unseen. Another terrifying howl rang out from above. It sounded like a soul in torment being bound into the form of a wolf.

"Another wolf-man is born," said a voice in the darkness. There was fear in it.

"Massimo will make us invincible," said another voice. "He brought Jaro back from the brink of death with his magic. His Wolves will drive the Sunlander bastards out of the mountains and Valkyria will be ours again."

The voice spoke with a sort of booming false confidence that told Kormak its owner was scared and as much trying to convince himself as anyone listening. That provoked laughter.

"I have not noticed you volunteering, Alyx," said the first voice. There was a sneer in it as well as laughter.

"I do my part. I don't need to give up my soul for the land of our fathers. I leave that to heroes." There was an ironic flourish on the word heroes. "We're both too old for that. Leave it to the young and stupid."

"I know what you mean," said the first speaker, "but I would not say it too loudly in camp."

"I won't but who can hear us here?" There was a sound of a flask being unstoppered and its contents gulped down then passed around. Kormak cursed. It seemed like they had chosen to pass through the area where Massimo's men slunk off to for a quiet drink. Alcohol was forbidden by many of the Lunar sects but such prohibitions had never bothered soldiers any, in Kormak's experience. He looked over at Petra, fearing she might do something very stupid but she was just lying there, eyes wide and fearful, mouth open. She was afraid and Kormak did not blame her.

After what seemed like a long time, the men took a piss and headed back to their camp.

He lay very still, and his heartbeat and his breathing seemed very loud to him until the steps had passed away into the night. They pushed on to the foot of the hill. Kormak was starting to think that this might not be the cleverest thing he had ever done. It was going to be tricky getting out of the valley even if he killed Razhak and Massimo.

Well, he would cross that bridge when he came to it.

"You're not taking the road then," said Petra. They stood at the foot of the rock on which the tower stood. It was not a sheer face, just very steep and rocky and it became steeper the higher you went.

"It will be watched."

"And so you're going to climb up the cliff and then the wall."

Kormak inspected it. "There's enough light, we should be able to get up there in less than an hour."

"If nobody spots us."

"That's true."

"Have you ever considered the fact that you might be insane?"

"Surprisingly, I have."

"Good because sane people don't say the sort of things you say quite as calmly as you say them."

"I can tell you're scared again because you are talking too much."

"Bloody right I am scared," said Petra.

"Then don't go on."

"Yeah. I'll just stay here in the middle of a moondog camp and wait for the sun to come up. What could possibly go wrong if I did that?"

"We're going to climb a small mountain and break into a castle full of man-wolves, a demon and a wicked sorcerer. What could go wrong with that?"

"Neither option is very attractive but I will make the best of a bad choice."

"That's very wise of you."

"There's no need to be sarcastic."

"I don't have time to stand here all night debating with you. I am going up. Follow me if you can."

"Follow you? I will be at the top before you."

She was good as her word. He had seen her climbing ahead of him, agile as a cliff-dwelling monkey, passing swiftly and silently while he struggled for a foothold, never faltering where he scrambled on dislodged stones and prayed they did not attract the attention of anyone below. He was breathing very hard and sweating by the time he pulled himself over the edge of the cliff and looked up at the walls of the tower.

"You are blowing like a horse after a ten mile gallop," Petra said with some satisfaction. "I thought you Aquileans could climb."

"Next time I'll let you wear my armour and carry my sword," Kormak said. "We'll see how you do."

She inspected the walls herself. "These are pretty hard. We could use daggers to spike our way up the wall but that would make a lot of noise."

"There's a postern gate over there."

"It'll be locked and guarded."

"I doubt it will be guarded. They are not besieged and they won't be expecting an invasion by an army of two."

"This Razhak knows you're after him and he will have told Massimo. Also this is a wizard's tower. It might be protected by magic."

"It might be but you heard the men in the valley. Massimo is working magic. I doubt he has the strength to create a wolf and set a ward at the same time."

"What about your friend, Razhak?"

"I doubt Massimo will let him cast any spells at all. He will be too worried by the consequences."

"You've thought this out, haven't you?"

"I had plenty of time while we were climbing the cliff."

"You got your breath back yet?"

"I never lost it."

"No. You were just letting me take a break, weren't you?"

"I am generous that way."

"You know how to open a postern gate?"

"I can slide a narrow blade through the gap at the edge of the door and lift the bar. If I can't, we have some more climbing to do."

"Let's get on with it then."

Kormak slid his dagger under the bar and lifted it up. He put his weight on the door and it swung open. There was a flight of stairs leading up: tight, narrow, spiralling and easily defensible. The sort of place where only one man could fight abreast at a time and a small group of defenders could hold a larger force for ages. He pushed on up them until he came to a landing, then paused and listened.

The howls and roars still echoed through the keep. He touched the Elder Sign on his chest. It was warm with the eddy currents of magic swirling around him. He put it back under his tunic so that if the magic became strong enough to light up the threaded moonsilver star in the talisman, it would not be visible and give his position away in the darkness.

Petra was behind him now, her knife in her hand. She moved cautiously and quietly along. Kormak stuck his head round the corner and looked along the corridor. It was empty. Torches flickered eerily, sending shadows dancing.

"Not a lot of guests here," said Petra. Kormak kept his mouth tightly shut and gestured for her to do the same. This was not the time or place for flippant jokes. A mistake here could cost them their lives.

What did she expect anyway? There was a reason why Massimo's army was camped in the valley below. Mortal men would not want to share the keep with a sorcerer and the monsters he was creating. Anyone they encountered here was likely to be strange and dangerous.

He stepped out into the corridor and began to walk confidently along it. He had long ago learned that just the sight of someone doing this in a place where they should not have been could disarm suspicion for crucial seconds.

The howls echoed through the corridors and seemed to resonate within his bones. He guessed that whoever Massimo was transforming was not enjoying the process. This sort of magic was rarely painless and always unpleasant. He followed the sounds as best he could, moving towards the centre of the keep.

Eventually, they came to what must once have been a temple chamber. There were still statues in alcoves around the walls. A series of inscribed Lunar circles intended to channel power had been etched into the floor and filled with moonsilver. It glowed as the light of the moon flooded the room through the open shutters in the ceiling. It illuminated a naked man chained to the altar. He was the one doing the howling.

Around the chamber men stood stone faced as sentries, their faces like stone, the effort of concealing their emotions engraved on their features. A youth with a more than passing resemblance to Petra watched as a tall, powerful man stood at the altar and chanted.

Massimo was robed all in black and his hair was jet black save for two patches of white at the temples. His beard was long and black with a badger stripe of white in it, and it flowed to his waist. In his hand he held a staff which was tipped with a silver crescent moon. Runes glowed along its length as he chanted. Witchfire danced from the staff to the chains holding the man as power was transferred from one to the other.

The cloying smell of essence of nightbloom incense filled the air, along with something else, the heady, hallucinogenic reek of powdered black lotus as it burned.

"That's Tam," Petra said, pointing to the youth standing beside the wizard. He stood full in the moonbeam and Kormak could see their faces had a family resemblance. He could have picked the youth out as her brother even if she had not told him.

Kormak unsheathed his sword.

"You're ready to kill someone now, aren't you?" Petra's voice was very quiet and he could hear the fear in it. The runes on his blade glowed. The amulet was warm against his chest. Powerful magic was at work here.

A shadow detached itself from a nearby wall. It belonged to a man. He had obviously seen Kormak. His outline blurred, there was strange stench in the air and suddenly he was larger than he had been, part man, part wolf. It opened its mouth and howled as it sprang.

The wolf-man's jaws were open, slaver dripped from its fangs. Its arms were outstretched to claw. Kormak stepped forward and struck. Its flesh sizzled as his blade bit through its neck and severed its head from its shoulders. Its still thrashing body flopped to the ground one way, its head rolled off in another. A pool of pink pus was already starting to surround the body as it transformed back.

More of the wolf-men bounded forward. Kormak counted at least six. The largest of them, a giant with a white ruff around its grey neck and bright mad eyes, howled and gestured and the pack bounded forward.

Kormak struck left and right, severing a limb, hacking through a chest. They slashed at him with their steel-hard claws, ripping his tunic, breaking links in his mail. He felt a pain in his side as one of them drew blood. Time and again they struck at him and he bounded to one side, chopping and stabbing as he weaved through their attacks, blocking blows with cuts that severed limbs and left wolf-men clutching at stumps.

It was obvious they were overconfident, not used to being hurt. They had never encountered anything that could break their magical protections before. One of them got close enough to try and rip out his throat with its great jaws. Kormak wedged his forearm between its jaws and brought his blade forward into its stomach. He heard it sizzle as it pierced flesh. The wolf-man howled this time in agony and Kormak pulled his arm free and punched it in the snout. It fell backwards.

In the interim two more Wolves had bounded forward. Each took him by the arm, claws digging into mail and threatening to tear through the leather undershirt. Kormak felt the enormous strength of the creatures and knew he was helpless against it. He allowed himself to fall backwards pushed by the creature's momentum. His sword dropped from his hand but he managed to get one arm free. He pulled out his amulet from beneath his tunic. The five pointed star of the Elder Sign glowed hot in its setting. He jammed it into the eye of one wolf-man. It let go as it roared and clutched its eye in a pain-filled gesture that was peculiarly human.

The other wolf-man had him by the throat. Kormak looked into its blazing hate-filled eyes and in that moment knew he was dead. The creature was stronger than he was and it was lowering its snout to rip out his throat. He threw all his strength against it, but it was useless, a child wrestling with an adult. Suddenly the wolf gave out a piercing, high-pitched scream of agony. The glowing runes of a dwarf-forged blade passed through its neck. The flesh burned where it touched and the wolf dropped Kormak. He saw Petra standing there, holding the blade in her hand.

"I did good," she said. "I'll make a Guardian yet."

"Maybe you will," Kormak said, snatching the blade out of her hand and bringing it down on the wolf-man that still clutched its wounded eye. He gazed around; there was only Massimo, Razhak and the pack leader now. Kormak smiled at them.

"Who wants to die next?" he asked. His smile was very cold.

Massimo stood illuminated in the moonbeams. He looked shocked. Tam looked appalled. The giant wolf-man leader did not look at all troubled. It flexed its huge arms and stretched its hands and long talons emerged from them. It opened its mouth revealing dagger-like teeth.

"You have slain Jaro's minions, Champion of the Sun," said Massimo. "But you will find Jaro is a completely different proposition. I used most of my magic to bring him back from the edge of death and filled him with the mightiest of the Shadow wolf spirits. He is the first and strongest of my creations. "

"He will be the last," said Kormak. His gaze flickered from Massimo to Tam to the giant wolf-man. It was hard to tell which was the more dangerous.

"Petra, don't let him kill me," Tam said. "The demon's gone. Massimo exorcised him and fed him to his Wolves. He is going to kill me next and feed me to the Wolves."

Tam's voice sounded plaintive. Kormak did not dare take his eyes from his enemies to see how Petra was responding. Tam sounded fearful and very believable. Kormak wondered whether Razhak would manage to play on the ties of blood with the girl and whether he would soon have an enemy at his back. It would not be the first time he had been in such a situation.

"You're not Tam, you're the thing that killed him," Petra said. Her voice sounded shaky and uncertain.

"No, sister, I am not. Please believe me. I don't want to die." Tam had started to edge closer to Petra by a circular route that did not take him within the reach of Kormak's blade. His arms were spread wide. His hands were open. He was the very picture of a frightened teenage boy. Kormak let him close the gap. Anything that put the demon within striking distance was good.

"It has been interesting," said Massimo. "Your blade is everything the tales say. I had not thought anything could wreak such havoc as you have among my creations, Guardian."

For a moment, Kormak's attention was split between Massimo and Tam. The giant wolf-man sprang. He was different from the others. He struck like a thunderbolt, sight-blurringly swift. His claws slashed forward and tore at the mail on Kormak's chest, popping rings, slashing leather. He had barely time to step back and launch a counter-blow. The giant avoided it easily and struck again, claw slashing at Kormak's shoulder. The force of the impact was like a sledge-hammer strike. Kormak wondered that nothing was broken.

"I told you, Guardian," Massimo said.

Kormak reeled back under the huge Wolf's savage onslaught. The wolf-man kept striking at him and hitting, too fast to be parried. Kormak realised that it was toying with him now, like a cat playing with a mouse. Out of the corner of his eye, he saw that Tam had reached Petra. His arms were outstretched to embrace his sister. She looked at him with tears running down her face. She looked torn between fear and gratitude, like a girl who had gotten her brother back and could not quite believe it.

"No," Kormak shouted as she reached forward to meet Tam. In that moment, a smirk passed over the youth's face that only Kormak could see, an expression, old and evil and inhuman that could not possibly belong to a human boy. Then his eyes widened, and he looked down to see the girl's dagger driven through his chest and blood pumping from the wound.

"Got you, you bastard," Petra shouted a look of triumph on her face.

"Get away from him now," Kormak shouted as the wolf-man came at him once more. Tam fell forward his hand outstretched, and one hand closed on the girl's shoulders. She spasmed and threw back her head to scream. A bright green glow appeared in Tam's eyes and flared brightly. A glow surrounded the pair and then the glow was in

Petra's eyes and Tam's decomposing form was lying on the ground. The girl now wore the evil expression, glanced in fear at Kormak and turned and ran from the chamber.

Kormak cursed. The wolf-man sprang back to the assault, a whirlwind of fanged death. It took all of Kormak's skill just to stay alive as he backed away from the furious beast. His spine was pressed to the wall and he could retreat no further. The wolf opened his mouth and howled again. Kormak leapt forward, stabbing with the sword, as the man-wolf launched himself into a spring. The wolfman's greater weight slammed Kormak into the wall even as it drove the blade into the monster's chest with additional force.

Stars danced before Kormak's eyes and all the wind was smashed out of his body. He smelled the monster's breath on his face even as he watched the light die from its eyes. He struggled to push himself upright as Massimo raced closer. It was a struggle pushing the wolfman's huge weight off but it became lighter by the second and pinkish pus leaked over Kormak as it transformed back into a large, handsome, silver-haired man.

"You killed me," Jaro said. He sounded as if he could not quite believe it. Kormak pulled himself upright just in time to confront Massimo. The wizard held his staff ready to strike. Kormak did not doubt there were potent and deadly spells woven into it. It would be best not to let it touch him, even wearing his protective amulets.

Massimo came to a halt and stared at Kormak. Fear and hate warred on his face. Kormak's legs felt as if they were about to give way. His body felt battered beyond belief. His chest felt as if it was on fire. He let none of his weakness show in his voice when he spoke, "There's just you and me left now," he said. "Soon there will be only me."

Massimo took a step back. He knew that physically he was no match for a Guardian, potent wizard though he might be. He needed time to weave his spells.

"There's no need for us to fight," the wizard said, his eyes darting around the temple. Was he expecting help to come, Kormak wondered? He doubted any men at arms would come to investigate the goings-on up here but perhaps Razhak would summon them. The thought of the demon and what he had done to Petra made Kormak snarl. He owed the girl his life and he had allowed her to die. Or worse. He took a step forward.

"I can help you find the demon," Massimo said. Kormak took another step forward. Massimo took another step back. They were walking towards the open balcony at the far end of the sacred space.

"I doubt it," Kormak said.

"It is hurt." Massimo said. There was an urgency in his voice as if he was desperate to convince Kormak that he had something to bargain with. "All the centuries stuck in the jar have weakened it, damaged it in some way. It does not have its full power and it needs to find new bodies or it will die from lack of energy."

Kormak took another step forward. Massimo moved away. "It told you this, did it?"

"Yes but it did not need to. I could tell just by studying its aura. It wanted my help. It wanted me to weave spells that would strengthen it before it made its journey."

"What did it offer you in return?" Massimo licked his lips. Sweat beaded his face.

"Secrets, many magical secrets. The Ghul knows much magic that has been forgotten in this modern age."

"And you were willing to help it in return."

"I do what I need to do to protect my people. Its knowledge would have been helpful."

"It will leave a trail of death across the lands. It has already begun to." Massimo's back was against the wall now. He held his staff out with both hands as if it could form a barrier between him and Kormak. He did not look so powerful or confident now, just a large, flaccid man with fear in his eyes.

"I can tell you where it is going," said Massimo.

"Oh you will," said Kormak. "One way or another. There are many ways to make a man talk and I know all of them." He kept his voice flat and emotionless. He knew it would sound more menacing that way.

"It's going to the dead city of Tanyth. It has to. It's where it was born. There are magical engines there that will heal it. If it does not, it will surely die and soon." Massimo was babbling now. The front of his robe was stained with urine. "Don't kill me," he said.

"You have committed crimes against the Holy Sun and his people. You have had commerce with demons. You have broken the Law. There can be only one penalty."

Massimo suddenly swung his staff at Kormak. It was what the Guardian had been waiting for. He parried the blow and stabbed forward. Massimo's flesh did not sizzle but he died like any other man would as Kormak's blade pierced his heart. Kormak looked up. The full moon gazed down on him mockingly. He turned and looked on the scene of carnage. Bodies were strewn all through the temple space. There was an army waiting in the valley.

Kormak stripped off the tunic that had belonged to the Wolves. No one had opposed him when he rode out of the valley. The sentries even answered his questions when he put them.

Yes, a girl had ridden through claiming she was a courier sent with instructions to the Wolves. She was heading east, along the main road, bound for Steelriver. Kormak doubled back and took the path to where his horse waited with what remained of his gear. It was a delay but some of the things in his saddlebags would prove useful and a second steed would do no harm in the pursuit. He knew where Razhak was going now. He knew what his present form looked like. He would follow and he would kill the demon and he would take revenge for Petra and her brother and the others it had killed.

It would not escape him, even if he had to follow it to the edge of the world

THE FLESH STEALER

"BE VERY STILL, stranger," said a voice from behind Kormak. The beam of a lantern fell on him, illuminating the hideously decomposing corpse he had been inspecting.

The highlander glanced up from the body of the murdered man, squinted down the alley, towards the light. There were two men there, wearing the conical helmets of the Vandemar city night watch. He said, "I am not the one you are looking for."

"We'll be the judge of that," said one of the watchmen. He was tall, almost as tall as Kormak and even broader although most his weight was fat. His massive form blocked one exit of the narrow alley.

He held a crossbow with the negligent ease of a man who knew how to use it and the bolt was pointed at Kormak's heart. Kormak doubted that even his mail shirt, forged by dwarves in the ancient days before they departed the surface world, would be able to stop it at this close range. He was in no hurry to find out. He had no intention of dying in this dark alley between the massive tenements of Vandemar if he could help it. He still had work to do.

"Step away from the body, stranger," said the big man's partner, the one holding the lantern. He was small and wiry and looked the smarter of the two by far. He rang his hand-bell loudly. "Keep your hands away from your sword. You have the look of a man who is quick with his hands but believe me you're not as fast as a crossbow bolt. No one is."

Kormak did as he was told. He kept his hands out from his sides and he made no sudden moves. "I tell you, you are making a mistake. There's not much time before the killer strikes again."

The weasel faced man grinned appreciatively. "It's good that you are so co-operative. Not many of those we pick up are. But I doubt the killer will be doing much killing while we have you here though."

"Look at the body then tell me that," said Kormak.

"Take a few steps back and I will do just that thing." He kept ringing the damn bell and Kormak knew it was only a matter of time before more watchmen came, even in this dingy run down part of the city.

Kormak backed away. The guard's eyes did not leave him. "What happened here, anyway?" he asked. "You and Ana come to some sort of arrangement? She lure this poor bastard up here and you knock him off? It won't be the first time but it'll be the first time she's been caught. You'll both swing for this."

"Ana?" Kormak asked.

"Don't play innocent. You know her. Red-haired trollop. This alley is her patch, has been for years. You her new pimp?"

Kormak grinned a wolfish grin. "I am a Guardian."

The guards laughed. "Sure and I am Our Lady of the Moon," said the bigger one of the two.

"You picked a strange place to step out of the old stories," said the smaller one. "I thought I had heard them all but this is a new one. Wait till we tell the lads down at the watch-house."

"I don't have time to argue," said Kormak. "Take a look at the body and then tell me that a mortal man did that."

The weasel faced man shrugged and squatted down by the body. He looked at it, looked up and then turned and bent double. The sound told Kormak that he was being sick.

"What did you do to him?" the small guard asked when he had finished dumping the contents of his stomach on a pile of offal. He stood up straight and began to jerk his warning bell frantically. Its loud clangour rang out through the alley, scaring even the rats that had started to gather for their feast.

"I did nothing," said Kormak. "The Ghul did it."

"A Guardian and a Ghul," said the big man. He was still chuckling. He had not inspected the body as closely as his companion. "This is an interesting tale for the lads."

His companion did not look amused now. He looked scared. "You a wizard, big man?" he asked. "You know some sort of Shadow magic?"

"No—I hunt those who do."

"Yeah and next you'll be telling us you kill the Children of the Moon as well."

"Not always," said Kormak. "Only when they break the Law and will not repent it."

"That's crazy talk," said the bigger guardsman. "It's the bedlam lockup for you, my friend."

"Look at the body then tell me I am crazy," said Kormak. He spoke slowly. He was starting to lose his patience. The big man kept laughing but the crossbow did not waver. His companion leaned forward and whispered something in his ear. He looked down then and he stopped laughing. As soon as their eyes were off him, Kormak sprang forward, lithe as a panther.

The crossbow swivelled. Kormak struck the side of it with his fist. The bolt flickered off down the alley, clattering against the wall. Kormak punched the big guard in his ample stomach, dropping him. A second blow sent the smaller man spinning into the wall. Kormak grabbed him, smashed his head against the wall until he fell. The big man was groaning and trying to unsling the club from his belt. Kormak kicked him in the head then raced off down the alley. He jumped a midden heap, vaulted over a low wall of crumbling brick and turned left, racing under ancient balconies and the wooden walkways that ran between the upper stories of the tenements.

The alleys were dark and dingy but he kept moving, knowing with every minute that passed his task was getting harder. It had been little more than luck he had found the body. A passing trader had described Razhak's last victim heading this way with a red-haired girl. Kormak had not been sure whether to believe him at the time but it was the only lead he had got so he took it and found the familiar looking corpse.

Razhak had stolen the form of pedlar called Nial after he had abandoned the form of the girl, Petra. Now, unless Kormak was greatly mistaken, the Ghul was wearing the body that had once belonged to Ana. He knew he had only a few hours before it stole another and left behind a hideously decomposing corpse.

Or it would if it was sensible. It knew Kormak was after it. He had almost caught it in Steelriver and in an inn along the Holy Road. It would want to make at least one more shift, to a body for which it would be much harder to find a description. That would make the task of finding it much more difficult, and the watch would be after him now and Kormak would be out of time.

He should have killed the watchmen. He would have bought himself some time by slitting the watchmen's throats. It was what Razhak would have done. The Ghul would leave no witnesses. He could not do that. The men had done him no harm. They were not his enemies. They were not creatures he was hunting. It was no part of his duty to kill men who were just doing theirs.

It was going to cost him though. Soon the watchmen would wake up with a grudge, and they would know what he looked like and what he sounded like. They might even be able to spot him by the way he wore his blade. He had told them he was a Guardian, after all, in the slight hope that they might aid him. Well, there was one thing he could do about that. He unbuckled the sword belt from around his chest, where it supported the scabbard at his left shoulder. He buckled it around his waist. He forced himself to walk more slowly as he approached the torchlit shambles of the Mall. He slouched his shoulders, and assumed a drunken, stumbling walk.

He emerged into an area that was comparatively well lit by flickering torches over the alley mouths and red-lanterns over the doors of the cathouses. Big men with hard-looking glances inspected him as he passed. Girls called for his custom. They smelled of alcohol and cheap scent. The cleaner, better looking ones were all in the bars and brothels. When they saw he was not interested, they left him alone and went in search of more attentive clients. There were plenty of those. Vandemar was where the Holy Road met the Great Silk Route. From its harbour ships bore the spices of Marathay and the silks of Vendalaya all the way to Taurea and the kingdoms of the

Sunlanders. From here Oathsworn Templars set out along the Holy Road to defend the Sacred Lands of the Sun.

The red light district was full of men from half a dozen Solari kingdoms. He saw massive Taurean warriors with full golden beards, garbed in the heavy armour of Templar Knights. There were dusky skinned magii from Skorpea and the hot lands of the Far South, robed in silk, carrying staffs carved from human bone. There were men wearing the silver crescent signs of moon-worshippers and the golden disks of those who followed the Holy Sun. A snake-charmer from Far Kothistan played his pipes in the street while his iridescently scaled pets danced to his wailing music, their poisoned fangs clicking shut close to the naked ankles of the fakir's diaphanously clad twirling wife.

There were more than just men present. Two green-haired elf-women walked passed. They studied him with huge almond shaped eyes, arms around each other's waists. One beckoned to him enticingly. He shook his head. A giant strode along, a noble-woman's palanquin strapped to his back, and a retinue of fork-bearded desert-born guards trailing in his wake.

Kormak saw two monstrous grey-skinned orcs, a head taller than he was and twice his weight. Just the sight of them made his hackles rise. He had fought in the orc wars and the idea of being able to pass them in the street was alien to him. One of the creatures saw him staring and grinned, showing its tusks, wrinkling the multi-coloured scar tattoos on its face. There was no mirth in the expression. To an orc a smile was a challenge. Kormak looked away, and heard the orc grunt contemptuously to its companion. A gobbet of spittle landed on his boots. Kormak forced himself to keep his hand away from his sword hilt and walked on.

A girl grabbed at his arm as he passed. "Looking for some company, mister?"

Kormak turned. The girl did not look like a typical street girl. She was not dressed so revealingly. Her face, though thin, was pretty and there was no makeup. Her eyes had a glint of humour in them and an alertness that made Kormak wary. "You know Ana?"

"You thinking of a threesome?"

"You know her or not?"

"A regular of hers, eh?"

"You seen her?"

"Big Ana: tall girl, red hair, white skin, freckles? Getting a bit old for the game?"

"That sounds like her. Can you tell me where to find her?" Kormak jangled his purse. "There's something in it for you, if you can."

The girl looked up and down the street. She did not seem particularly busy. She stuck out a slender hand with bitten nails. "Hand it over."

Kormak gave her one of his silver pieces. It was the ancient type, with a hole in the middle, meant to be strung on cords around the neck. She looked at it in the torchlight, held it up to her eye and laughed. "This is three hundred years old," she said. "Reign of Albigen the Third. Where did you get it?"

"Give it back if you don't want it?"

"I want it. I could sell this to a collector. Got any more? We could split the difference on what Miser Tala pays me."

"I am looking for Ana," Kormak said. "Tell me where she is. It's important."

The girl looked at him and shook her head. "You got it bad for her, eh? Who would have guessed?"

"Yes. I really want to find her," said Kormak. "You going to tell me or you going to give me the coin back?"

"You said there was more if I could tell you."

"If you tell me true, I'll give you another of those but I need to find her fast."

"I'll show you where she is then and you can hand over the gelt."

The girl turned and walked along ahead of him, pausing occasionally to make sure he was still there. Kormak wondered if he was making a mistake trusting her. After all, she could be making this up or she could be thinking of the wrong girl entirely. He shrugged. What choice did he have? This was the only lead he had and if it was wrong he would need to find another way to pick up the trail. He had already followed it too long. One way or another he was going to end this tonight.

"Where you from?" the girl asked. "Not from around here, I can tell."

"Aquilea."

"That's somewhere far west, isn't it? An island on the verge of the Outer Ocean where the great waterfall drops of the Edge of the World."

"It's a mountain land north of Taurea, keep heading north from there and you'll reach the Plains of Ice."

"The way I heard it," the girl said, "head north from anywhere and you'll hit the Plains of Ice eventually."

"I heard that too."

"So you're a westerner then. You're a long way from home. Trading in spice and silks I suppose, looking for a ship back."

She was fishing for information, he knew. Trying to figure out how much he was worth. A thought struck him. "Lead me into a robber's lair, girl, and you and your friends will all die."

She laughed in his face. "You're that tough, eh?"

"Tough enough," he told her.

She stopped laughing and looked closely at his scarred face. "Yes, I believe that," she said. "You're older than I thought at first and I'm guessing you did not get those grey hairs and those scars by being anybody's easy mark. What you do anyway? Mercenary?"

"Soldier," he said.

"You sworn to one of the Warlords then?"

"You always ask so many questions?"

"Only when I like the look of a man . . . or I think he's wealthy."

"Which is it in my case?"

"A little of both."

It was his turn to laugh. "You're honest at least."

"You still want to find Ana?"

He nodded.

"Then here we are." They had paused outside a three story caravansary inn. The sign of some long sort of blue-scaled dragon hung over the doorway.

"The Blue Wyvern," the girl said. "Ana always goes here when she has some money. Scar the Orc deals her glitterdust and other things. I saw her head this way earlier. She looked a little dazed so I guessed she was coming down and looking to score again." She held her hand out. "Well, it's been sweet," she said. "Pay up and I'll be heading along."

"I still haven't found Ana yet. Wait here and I'll go in. When I come back out, you'll get paid."

"Oh yeah, sure I will. Maybe you would like to sell me the Pale Wizard's Tower while you are at it."

"You don't get paid until I find Ana."

"Then I am coming in with you."

"That might not be the wisest thing." She tilted her head to one side.

"Like that is it? You going to give her trouble, big man?"

"She inside or not?"

"I'm going in. You owe me another coin."

Kormak shrugged. "Don't say I didn't warn you."

"What's your name, big man? In case, I need to find you again?"

"Kormak. What's yours?"

"Nuala."

They walked up the stairs and through the swing doors of the tavern. The bouncers looked at Kormak but did not say anything. They looked harder at the girl. It seemed as if one of them recognised her and was about to say something.

"She's with me and I have gold," said Kormak. He slipped the man a coin.

"The customer is always right," said the bouncer. They went inside.

"You go into these places a lot?" Nuala asked.

"I've been in a few."

"I could tell." Kormak strode up to the bar and put a coin on the counter-top. "Beer for me and whatever my friend here is having. And have one yourself," he said.

The barman poured two drinks and put a coin in the goblet on the stand behind him. "For later," he said. "The boss does not like it if we drink on the job."

"Understandable," Kormak said. "Ana come in?"

"Ana who?"

Kormak tapped another silver coin on the counter-top. "Tall girl, red hair likes glitterdust, knows Scar. Would you like me to draw you a picture?"

The barman looked over at the bouncers. There were two more by the door.

"I'm not looking for trouble," Kormak said. "I need to find her fast though."

He put the coin on the counter-top and placed another beside it, setting it spinning with a flick of his thumb.

"You a friend of hers?"

"A special friend. A client."

The barman trapped the coin with his hand. "She went upstairs to see Scar. She looked a bit stunned."

"He'll give her something to perk her up, no doubt," Kormak said.

"No doubt."

Kormak put another coin on the bar, finished his drink and said, "Maybe he'll give me the same."

The barman gave him a professional smile. "You can but ask," he said. His gaze went to the first floor balcony. An orc was coming out. With him was good-looking, blowsily dressed red-head. She looked down and pointed at Kormak and shrieked. "That's him, Scar. That's the bastard who said he'd cut my throat."

The orc followed her pointing finger. Kormak cursed and began walking towards the stair. Two bouncers moved to block his way.

"You don't want to do that," he said.

"No choice, pal," said the biggest of the two. "You don't pay our wages. Scar does and she's a client of his."

He smiled as he spoke but before he finished the sentence a blow was on its way towards Kormak's head. Something glittered on the man's fist. Metal knuckle-dusters, Kormak assumed. He stepped to one side and inside the man's guard and dropped the man with a punch. His twisted and his elbow buried itself in the second bouncer's stomach. The man fell retching. Kormak took the stairs two at a time. The red-head kept screaming. "Stop him. He'll kill me!"

The rest of the bouncers and the clients rushed at Kormak. The orc drew two black steel scimitars. It was not a good sign. Such weapons were the mark of an orcish blademaster. Forged in the blood furnaces of the shaman smith's they would resist even the bite of a dwarf-forged blade without notching. Kormak wondered if he could put a knife through Ana's throat from the distance. The orc fell into a guard position. It was much bigger than Kormak.

"I don't want to kill you," Kormak said.

The orc laughed. Its tusks glistened in the lantern-light.

As soon as they crossed blades, Kormak knew he was fighting against a master. The orc was astonishingly fast, skilled and strong. Scar smiled as he brought his blades into play and for a few seconds Kormak was hard put to defend himself. He saw by his opponent's face that he was not the only one surprised. After a few moments the orc frowned and then gave the slightest nod of acknowledgement, as much to himself as to Kormak, that he faced a worthy foe.

"I shall eat your heart and your liver," Scar said. "You are worthy."

Kormak saw Razhak begin to slide away from behind the drug dealer and move towards the further staircase. He cursed, determined that the stealer of flesh would not escape him again.

A faint look of contempt passed across Scar's face. He obviously thought he was the subject of Kormak's words. Kormak heard feet on the stairs behind him. He knew it was only a matter of heartbeats before the bouncers were on him and there was no way he could defend himself from them and a warrior of Scar's skill.

He adjusted his breathing as he had been taught so long ago on Mount Aethelas and unleashed the full fury of his sword arm. Scar went immediately on to the defensive, stepping back and away, defending himself in a whirlwind of blades. Knowing it was risky, but that he had to chance it anyway, Kormak vaulted over the balcony, and landed, knees flexing to take the strain of the fall on a table on the lower floor. Drinks spilled and chairs overturned as patrons scrambled to get away, taken aback by the sudden eruption of a large swordsman in their midst.

Razhak had reached the bottom of the stair and pulled up short, aware that he was going to have to confront the Guardian after all. A look of fear flickered over the face of the female form he wore. Kormak tensed himself to spring when Scar vaulted down from the balcony to land atop the table between him and Razhak.

"It has been a long time since I have had the pleasure of fighting one almost my equal, stranger. Who was your master?"

The dealer stood as ready to fight as talk and Kormak knew that his time was running out. Out of the corner of his eye, he could see the man behind the bar was loading a crossbow. It would be a tricky shot in the crowded bar but all it would take would be a lucky hit and it would all be over. Worse, Razhak was already making her way out through the back way and not only Scar but a room full of panicking patrons now lay between them.

"I do not fight for pleasure," said Kormak.

"Then fight for your life," said Scar and sprang. Kormak found himself pressed face to face with the orc, glaring into its red eyes, able to count the stitches of its scar tattoos. The table shuddered under their combined weight. They measured strength against strength for a moment then Kormak attempted to trip the orc. Springing back, Scar landed on the space between the tables, keeping his feet lithe as a cat. He lashed out at Kormak's leg. The Guardian sprang above the blow, letting it pass beneath him, knowing it was a mistake since it would put him off balance.

Scar struck again and somehow Kormak twisted to parry the blow. He landed badly, losing his balance and rolled away, feet over shoulders, using his momentum as he had been taught. He heard Scar bellowing at the tavern patrons to get out of his way. He smelled burning now. Someone had knocked over a lantern in the confusion. More people were screaming. The crowd was starting to panic.

He felt a hand on his shoulder and turned ready to strike. He saw Nuala. She tugged at him and pointed towards the door. He saw the sense in what she was saying. There was no point in staying to fight against overwhelming odds; nothing to be gained either. He nodded and shouldered his way towards the doorway, with her following behind. He punched a man down who got in his way, barged another to one side and moments later they were outside.

"Scar needs help, Fat Bulo and his men attacked," said Nuala. The bouncers nodded and made their way through the doorway adding to the confusion.

"Come on, let's get out of here," said the girl. "I think you've caused enough trouble for one night."

"The trouble is just starting," Kormak said. "And I am not the cause of it."

"You weren't kidding when you said you were good with a sword," said Nuala. "I don't think I have ever seen anyone last so long against Scar. He is the best swordsman in the city, possibly excepting the champions of the Four Warlords."

"He was skilled," said Kormak. He glanced around warily. Their surroundings were enough to give anyone pause. It was a small, hole-in-the-wall drinking den, deep within the maze of alleys around the Mall. It was little more than a bench, some planks set on beer barrels and a canvas canopy overhead. All around were more tables where people ate and drank. They were surrounded by the bustle of people.

"You have a gift for understatement, stranger," she said. "They say Scar was the First Blade of the Red Horde. He would still be today perhaps, had he not plotted against the Khan of Khans."

"Who tells this story, Scar?"

"It's no joke. He's killed two score of men since he came to the city, made himself the most feared gang boss in the Mall and you have contrived to make him your enemy."

"It's a gift I have, apparently."

"It does not seem to trouble you all that much. Is your life worth so little to you?"

"I have a job to do here, girl, and I intend to see it done."

"A job that involves killing some pox-raddled old whore? How can that be important enough to throw your life away?"

"The woman Ana is dead. She has been possessed by a demon." Nuala looked at him again. Her eyes narrowed. She tilted her head to one side. She looked as if she were trying to judge whether he was sane or not.

"A demon is loose in our city? Which of the sorcerers unleashed it? Mandragora? Khane? And why? They are not normally so careless. They know the Warlords would have their head."

"None of them. I have followed this demon all the long leagues from Belaria. It flees before me, sometimes, turns at bay at others. Somehow I feel we are reaching the end of the road here, one way or the other."

"You certainly will, if you offend the likes of Scar."

"If it is so dangerous, why are you still here?"

"Because you still owe me money." She smiled as she said it. It lit her face, made her pretty in a way Kormak had not noticed before. He found himself smiling back.

"That is a matter soon settled. It might be best for you if you left me."

"It might, but I can see that you might need some help soon and you look like a man who can pay well for it."

"What sort of help can you give me in my task?"

"You might be surprised."

"I am serious. This is not a game, girl. You could get killed. Or worse."

"Worse than being killed? I am not one of those women who believe in fates worse than death."

"Razhak could devour your soul, and steal your flesh."

"How do you know this?"

"I belong to the Order of the Dawn."

"I thought they were a legend. I had heard they were all dead."

"Not all of us. Not yet."

"And that is why you hunt this demon across the world?"

"I swore an oath. And I keep my promises. For good or ill."

She tilted her head to one side. Her look was wary and watchful. It reminded him of a nervous bird considering taking flight. "Either you are the most convincing maniac I have ever met or you are serious."

"I am not a madman." He did not know why he was bothering to try and convince her of it. He had work to do and Razhak was getting no easier to find, and yet somehow, he found inertia creeping over him. It has been a long time since he had talked at length with anyone, let alone a pretty woman.

"Tell me about this demon."

"Why? Are you a sorcerer?"

"No but I know one. He might be able to help you."

"Wizards are rarely friendly to my order."

"This one will be friendly to anyone if they have enough cash."

"What good can he do me?"

"How do you propose to find this demon now? Will you go hunting through the city while Scar and his men hunt you?"

"If need be."

"That's your plan? It's not a very good one."

"Alas, I find my options are limited."

"Then what harm will it do to consult my friend? He is a diviner. He may be able to help."

"And this will of course cost me . . ."

"Well, I should be paid for the matter of the introduction and he will need money. As I said, he is fond of gold."

Kormak looked up. The watchmen he had encountered earlier had entered the courtyard. They were looking around and he did not doubt they were looking for him. He put his head down and kept his hand on his sword.

"What is it?" Nuala asked.

"The watch," he said. "They are looking for me. I gave them those bruises earlier."

She rose and he thought she was about to take flight. He would not have blamed her. Instead she moved around to where he sat and wriggled onto his knee. Looking over her shoulder he could see the watchmen coming ever closer. In a few heartbeats they would be close enough to recognise him for sure and he could not fight them with the weight of a woman on his lap.

She leaned forward and said, "Be still. This won't hurt," then kissed him full on the lips. He was momentarily startled and then he realised what was happening. His face was obscured from view. They looked just like any other street girl and customer in the place. The watchmen certainly would not be expecting this of a Guardian hunting a demon. It was not what he expected himself. He found himself kissing her back and the embrace lasted longer than was strictly necessary for cover.

Once the watchmen had passed, she stood up, looking at their receding backs, then stretched out her hand to him. She pulled him from the seat towards the shadows, the very picture of a street girl leading a client to a private place to fulfill an assignation. Kormak wondered if perhaps that was what was really going on here, then he shook his head as his habitual wariness re-asserted itself. It would not do to trust this woman, even a little, he decided.

She laughed as they made their way through the alleys. "Scared for your virtue, noble knight?" she asked.

"I was just wondering how much you were going to charge me for the kiss." She paused for a moment. Her face suddenly looked hard then she laughed. "I did that for fun. I have no love of the watch and you are a handsome man."

"I am not that handsome."

"Then let us say you have the type of ugliness that does not repel me."

"I am flattered."

"No, you are not. This sort of thing happens to your sort all the time. The enigmatic stranger, passing through on his way to somewhere else."

"You sound like you have had experience."

"So do you." What could he say? She was right.

Silence fell as she led him through the maze of alleys. He was starting to suspect it was true. If Vandemar was not the most populous city in the world it must be pretty close. He had never been in slums so extensive or so tightly packed. It seemed like a lot of people were packed within these walls. He shuddered to think what Razhak could do in such a crowded place.

"What are you grunting about?" Nuala asked.

"I was thinking I don't think I have ever seen a city so densely populated."

"A lot of people have crowded in from the countryside over the past few years. They think they can avoid the wars of the Warlords that way, the pillaging armies. They think that they can make their fortune in the great merchant city, that the streets are paved with gold."

The bitter way she said the words made him wonder if she was one of those people who had fled from the countryside. He was not familiar enough with the local accents to tell whether she was local or not. "How did you get on the trail of this demon anyway?"

Was there fear in her voice? Perhaps what he had said earlier was starting to sink in.

"It killed a man called Nial in the caravansary at Lemal back along the Holy Road from Belaria. It took his body and left a stinking corpse. Before that it stole the form of a girl called Petra. I knew her somewhat."

"A friend?"

"In a way."

"How can you be so certain you are on the right track?"

"It follows the Holy Road. It is heading for Tanyth out beyond Sunhaven in the Sacred Lands. I had hoped to catch it before it made it so far. I was unlucky. So far it has always managed to elude me."

She laughed. "I have never met a man who thought it unlucky not to meet a demon."

"If I find it, I can kill it. There are few of its kind I cannot, if I am lucky."

"A man of your talents could make a good living in this part of the world, providing you did not upset the wrong people, of course. Given your personality you would probably have a very short career."

"I never expected my life to be a long one."

"Then why do it?"

"I told you: I swore an oath."

"Somehow I doubt it is that simple."

"It's not. It never has been."

"You still trying to keep the mystery in our relationship."

"We don't have a relationship."

"And here was me thinking we were becoming friends."

"What's your story? You're not a flower-girl, are you?"

She shrugged. "No. No. I am not."

"Then what do you do?"

"I get by."

"Pickpocket? Bawd? Hustler?"

"You don't have a high opinion of me, do you?"

"I am trying to guess what a young woman your age is doing alone in the streets of the red light district at this time of night, if she is not a flower-girl."

"All three of the things you mentioned and some other things too," she said. "I know people. I put people in touch. I get people things that they want. I find out interesting things and exchange those with interested parties."

"You've a number of sidelines then . . ."

"A girl needs to get by."

"Do yourself a favour then, girl and don't try and pick my pocket. Do right by me and I'll see its worth your while. Do me wrong and I'll see you pay for it. On that you have my word."

"And you're the man who always keeps his promises," she said.

"Yes," he said. "I am."

"Here we are," Nuala said. They had stopped in front of a tall, narrow-fronted building so rickety it seemed in danger of imminent collapse. Huge beams had been spread between it and the building on the other side of the alley, seemingly in an attempt to prevent that from happening.

"I can see your friend is successful in his trade," Kormak said.

"There's no need to be so ironic. Darien is not that interested in the trappings of success. He is not materialistic."

"I am guessing he will still want my money though."

"He needs to pay for his research. All those books and alchemical ingredients cost money. He likes his wine and other things too."

She walked down a very narrow flight of steps disappearing below ground level. She began to rap on a metal door-knocker. Voices shouted from the windows for her to keep the noise down. A light went on within the cellar. Kormak heard someone move closer to the door, grumbling and cursing. He held himself ready. If there was going to be any treachery it would come now.

A slot in the door opened. There was a muttered exchange and obviously Nuala was recognised for the door opened. A tall, thin man, dressed in a none-too-clean robe stood there. He held a small saucer with a guttering candle on it. He looked up the stairs at Kormak and beckoned for him to come down. The Guardian did so slowly. The man did not look very threatening but if he was a wizard that meant nothing. They could be dangerous even when their hands were empty.

"Come inside, man," the wizard said. "I do not intend to stand out here all night while you decide to take a swing at me."

Kormak strode closer, still wary. Close up, Darien looked even less menacing. He was tall and thin and scruffy looking and smelled as if he had not washed in many days. There was wine on his breath and the scent of something else, possibly black lotus, one of the many narcotics to which mages became addicted because they believed it enhanced their powers and their ability to study ancient texts. Kormak began to suspect he knew why Darien had need of money. He did not relax his guard any. He had spent a lifetime in dangerous places with dangerous people where appearance was often deceptive, and wizards had a tendency to be among the most deceptive of all.

"A Guardian, eh?" Darien said. "And that would be a dwarf-forged blade, I suppose."

It came to Kormak that the man had a Sunlander accent and close up he looked like a Sunlander too.

"You are not from around here, are you?" Kormak asked.

"I am from Sideria, the port of Trefal, and I can see you are an Aquilean. I am surprised that you claim you are a member of the Order of the Dawn."

"You're not the first," said Kormak. He was oddly pleased to hear a familiar accent speaking a familiar tongue. He quashed the feeling. Now was not the time to relax his guard. "How did you end up here?"

"Same way as everybody else—I came to search for the mystic secrets of the east. I wound up without the price of passage home, and to tell the truth, this is as good a place as any for a man in my profession. Excellent book dealers, a long history of mystical and astrological research, some interesting systems of thaumaturgy . . . there's a lot to learn and a lot to write down. When I get back home I will have the material to astound the old men at the Colleges of Magery."

As soon as he heard the words, Kormak knew that Darien would never go home. He had just found a delusion to give his life in this distant place meaning. "You trained at the Siderian College then?"

"Yes. I studied under Wigge and Thalman. I was considered quite a promising mage once, you know." Some remnant of a once-fierce pride smouldered in his voice.

"I hope you have kept your skills honed. Nuala says you are a diviner."

Darien laughed. "I cast horoscopes for wealthy old women." He gave the girl a pointed look. "I perform divinations for those who wish to ascertain whether certain residences are protected by magic. It is a way of earning a crust. It is not my real work."

"That is a pity, for I have need of someone who truly has the gift."

"You are looking for someone or something."

"I am looking for a Ghul."

Darien slumped chair. He looked pale. He leaned over and poured himself a drink out of an alembic sitting on his workbench. "You seek one of the Undying ones. You have set yourself quite a task, man who calls himself a Guardian."

"I know it. I have followed this one from Belaria. I intend to follow him no further if I can help it. Can you help me?"

"I don't see why I should. Those creatures are dangerous, more dangerous than I think you can possibly understand."

"Few know more than I."

"Said with the confidence of the true ignoramus," said Darien.

"If you are too afraid to help me I will go and seek the thing myself. I understood you had need of gold."

"The dead and the damned have no need of gold and I might be both very soon if I went seeking a Ghul. They eat souls and steal flesh you know."

"A wizard who can tell me what any street-corner storyteller knows—how useful." He looked at Nuala. "I thought you said your friend was a scholar."

Nuala shrugged. "He is. He is not normally so backward when the prospect of earning is dangled in front of him either."

"The child seeks to tell her elders how to behave," Darien said. "Girl, if what this man says is true, I advise you to walk out the door and don't look back. Leave the city if you hear of any strange deaths. I most certainly will."

"There are always strange deaths in Vandemar," Nuala said.

"Newly dead bodies that look and smell like month old corpses, the worms wriggling through them even as the body decomposes?"

"I have not seen any."

Kormak nodded. It was clear that in this Darien actually knew what he was talking about. "I have seen one tonight," he said. "There will be another before morning unless I miss my guess."

Darien looked at him, clearing judging Kormak as much as the Guardian was judging him. "Why?" he asked. "The Ghul will not need to shift for at least another moon unless the body it currently occupies is sickly. They can dwell within a new form for years sometimes until they burn out all its life force."

"This one will want to avoid me. It knows I know what its current form looks like. Also it is damaged. It has just been freed from one of Solareon's amphorae after millennia."

"And naturally it fears you." The tone was mocking but Kormak could see the wizard was starting to take him seriously.

"It fears the sword I carry."

"The stories say Guardians carry magical blades," said Nuala.

Darien looked at her and laughed. "Is that why you are interested in him, girl? If so, let me give you a piece of advice you had best heed. No one ever got rich stealing a Guardian's blade. They always claim them back. Kill this one and they will send two more just as deadly and they will never rest until they have what is theirs. You do not wish to cross the Order of the Dawn in matters such as this."

"I was not thinking of any such thing," said Nuala, perhaps a little too quickly. Darien's smile widened.

"No. I would not have to be a diviner to see that you have something else on your mind, girl. Well, it's your funeral."

"You will not help?" Nuala asked. "You can find this thing if you want to. There is nothing you can't find with your spells and your crystals. You have told me so yourself often enough."

"What I say when I am in my cups and what I choose to do when I am stone cold sober are two different things, girl. This man is what he claims to be. You had best avoid him. His sort carry death with them wherever they go. It can be contagious."

"If you truly are a diviner, you could help me find this thing and kill it," Kormak said.

"I truly am but I would like to go on living."

"You might not get to do that if you don't help me."

"Was that a threat?" Suddenly the wizard, without changing in the slightest, seemed a lot more dangerous. His presence filled the room. His voice crackled with ominous menace.

"There is a Ghul loose in the city. It will take lives and cause havoc. You might be one of its victims."

"My premises are warded."

"And you never have to leave?"

The wizard considered him for a moment and seemed to weigh the possibilities. He poured himself another drink and then shook his head.

"I can get you passage back to the west," Kormak said. The wizard looked up. His interest was piqued now. "I can get you into the King's Library in Taurea."

"Could you now? Your Order still has some sway in Taurea, after all."

"Can you find the Ghul?"

"If you take me to where the last body was, yes."

"Will you?"

"For the price of passage west and a letter of introduction to the King of Taurea's librarians? Yes. On one condition. You protect me from this Ghul, come what may?"

"Very well."

"I have your word on that."

"You have my word."

"Then let us be about this business."

They retraced their steps back through the Mall, heading for the alley Kormak had fled earlier in the evening. He was muffled by a robe he had borrowed from the wizard and his face was hidden by one of the local mortarboard caps. He doubted he would have made a very convincing wizard's apprentice even without the sword on his hip but it was the best they could do.

There were watchmen everywhere and they seemed alert. There were bravoes that Nuala made them turn aside to avoid as well. "Scar's allies," she said. "The bouncers recognised me earlier and know I came with you. They will have passed that on to the orc by now."

"What are you going to do about that?" Kormak asked.

"I'll work something out. I may have to leave town for a while. If worst comes to worst, I'll tell the truth."

"The Holy Sun forbid you be driven to such a dire expedient! What truth would that be?"

"That you were just some stranger who paid me to show him the way to his place. By the way, when will you pay me?"

"When this is done and I have found out whether your friend is worth his fee. I have not decided yet whether this is not some sort of elaborate trick to part me from my money the two of you cooked up."

"You are one of those tiresome men who insists on paying by results I can see."

"I have found it is the one sure way of getting them."

"That is certainly a point in the method's favour."

"When you two have finished flirting perhaps you will tell me when we have found the place we are looking for," Darien said. "I am starting to catch a strange scent in the air."

Kormak looked at the wizard with new respect. They were close to the spot where he had found Nial's body. Another turn of the corner and they were there. The corpse was still present as well. Kormak had guessed that no one had wanted to go near the thing fearing it cursed or plagued or worse. The look of the wasted form did not trouble Darien. He walked right over to the corpse and bent over it. Kormak did the same, being careful as the wizard was not to step into the puddle of black putrescent matter surrounding it.

"Definitely a Stealer of Flesh," said Darien. He sounded at once frightened and oddly satisfied. "The signs of abandoned possession are all there: the withered corpse, the bites of a million worms, the oily liquid residue, the smell of exhumation. One of Death's children has been here and that's for sure."

He closed his eyes and intoned a chant in High Hardic. He kept at it for several long minutes, moving his head from side to side and sniffing the air. "It left here wearing the body of a woman."

"So much I already told you," Kormak said.

"Perhaps you would care to tell me where it is now," Darien replied. "Or would you just let me perform the task for which you are paying me?"

"Pray proceed." The wizard straightened up and partially opened his eyes, keeping them slitted as if he was squinting into some bright light. Kormak wondered how much of this was part of the spell and how much was just for show. He sometimes felt that even the wizard's themselves could not tell. Darien began to pace down the alley that Kormak had taken earlier, sniffing the air. He took a different turn from the one Kormak had, but shortly thereafter he was out in the streets of the Mall and heading towards the Blue Wyvern.

"How could this demon have known to find Scar?" Nuala asked. "Did it steal Ana's memories as well as her flesh?"

"They can and they do," said Darien. "They can accumulate a lot of strange knowledge over the years. This is why some sorcerers deal with them. Of course, they are Old Ones. They have much magical knowledge anyway."

"You know a lot about such things," said Kormak. He could not keep the suspicion out of his voice. He knew that Razhak was not a true Old One. Perhaps Darien did not.

"I am a wizard. It is my job to know such things and much strange knowledge comes to me as a byproduct of my researches."

"Why would an Old One steal human bodies?" Nuala asked. She spoke quietly so that they would not be overheard. Darien replied in a murmur.

"No one knows. Many of the sages have theories. Some say they wanted to hide among humans when the ancient wars that drove the Old Ones from the Lands of Men began, that they were spies sent among us to sow distrust and dissension.

"Malius says the Ghul were not true Old Ones at all but rather a slave race who sought to emulate their masters and divorced their spirits from their bodies. He claims that the process was imperfect and that the lost souls needed to find new housing simply in order to survive." Darius looked at Kormak as he said this.

"That would fit with what I have observed," Kormak said. "Razhak does not leave mortal form for longer than it takes him to jump from one body to the other. He seems to need the flesh in order to survive."

"Fascinating," said Darien. "There is a monograph to be written on this subject."

"Only if we survive the encounter," said Nuala.

"There is no need for you to be here, girl," said Darien. "It might be better if you are not. If our Guardian here succeeds in killing the body this demon wears it will be looking around for a new host. The less candidates there are present the better."

Nuala looked as if she was considering the wizard's words. Kormak would not have blamed her for departing. "I will pay you for what you have done," he said. "You have earned at least part of your fee. We can meet back at Darien's sanctum after we are done and I will settle all scores."

The girl looked at him and shook her head. "I have come this far. I will see this through to the ending. I am curious now."

"We all know what curiosity did to the cat, girl," said Darien.

"I am not a cat," she said.

"I know women who would disagree with that statement," said Darien.

"Not for very long," said Nuala.

"Not once you have shown them your claws anyway." Darien sniffed the air and closed his eyes and murmured something again. "The scent is getting much stronger."

"I am not surprised, we are getting very close to the Blue Wyvern," Nuala said.

"Let us move around the building," Darien said. "I will see if I can pick up the trail."

"Let's try and keep out of sight," Nuala said. "It would not do for Scar's bravoes to see us."

Darien nodded and they made a sweep around the outside of the tavern, sticking to the alleys, trying to be as inconspicuous as possible. By the end of it, Darien was frowning.

"What is it?" Kormak asked.

"The trail leads in to the Blue Wyvern."

"I already know that."

"It does not go out."

"So Razhak is still within."

"It seems the most likely option. You seem surprised."

"I would have expected the demon to take a new form and flee."

"Perhaps it has come to some accommodation with Scar. They would have something to offer each other."

"It would be a dangerous pact for Scar to make."

"He lacks your specialised knowledge on the subject of Ghuls, or mine for that matter."

"There is another possible explanation," Nuala said. Kormak and the wizard looked at her.

"Razhak knows you will come back for her. She may have told Scar this. They might be waiting for you within. If they are sensible, they may even have watchers set already. You are most likely walking into a trap, Guardian."

Kormak looked at the wall surrounding the Blue Wyvern. "I am going to have to go back in there, it seems."

"I trust you are not planning on doing so through the front door," said Darien. "That would seem particularly lacking in sense."

"I can get you in," said Nuala. "We go over the lock and up the cornices and in through the balcony on the third floor. All the lower windows are barred."

"It sounds like you've given this some thought on a previous occasion," said Kormak.

"Nuala can't look at a house without thinking of a way in through the window," said Darien, ignoring the glare the girl gave him.

Kormak considered his options. At least, he knew where the Ghul was, if Darien was telling the truth. The question was whether Razhak had changed forms once again and how to find him once he was in the building. Still, it was better than he had feared. At least he did not have to chase the demon through the city, looking for a trail of destroyed corpses. Of course, there were some unpleasant potential implications of the fact that the Ghul had decided to stay in one place as well. It was perhaps expecting him, and it had, perhaps, cut some sort of deal with Scar. Nuala was right. He might well be walking into a trap. He noticed that both the girl and Darien were staring at him.

"Well, what do you want to do?" the girl asked.

"I am going in."

"I am going with you. You don't look like you know how to take out a pane of glass without making a noise. Or are you planning on just smashing a window and hacking your way through Scar's men?"

"The thought had crossed my mind."

"All that will get you is dead and your demon will still be on the loose."

"Very well then," said Kormak. "Let's get going."

They made their way up to the wall. It was tall enough so that Kormak could reach the lip of the wall by stretching, but broken glass and nails had been set in the stonework on the top.

Nuala removed her leather jerkin and wadded it up. "Boost me up," she said.

Kormak made a stirrup of his hands and lifted the girl. She threw the jerkin over the sharp objects and then used it to stand on as she crossed. Kormak pulled himself up with his fingers and scrambled over with less grace than the girl. He felt as if the glass had punctured the jerkin in places but the garment had served to reduce any damage to mere scratches on his own clothing.

Nuala reached up and pulled the jerkin down. She opened it up, revealing slices and punctures in several places. "You'll pay for that," she said.

"I suspected I was going to," Kormak said.

"It's my favourite," she said, as if that explained everything, and perhaps it did to her. She glanced around. The garden looked empty and there were no guards anywhere in sight. They padded across it, keeping to the shadows.

"I always expect black lions in places like this," whispered Nuala.

"Not very convenient when you have clients coming and going and the neighbours might complain," Kormak said.

"There is that."

They reached the wall. Kormak could see what Nuala had meant. Rows of gargoyles were carved on the side of the building from the second floor. She reached within her jerkin and produced a coil of rope. It looked as thin as string and Kormak doubted it would hold their weight. That did not seem to bother Nuala as she coiled it into a noose and then threw it over the nearest gargoyle.

"Spidersilk," she said and began to clamber up the line. "It's strong enough to hold both of us, although I suggest you don't put that to the test unless you absolutely have to." She reached the first gargoyle, grasped it and pulled herself up. That put her within reach of another gargoyle and she just kept climbing. Kormak decided he had better follow her.

In armour, it was not quite as easy as the girl made it look but he managed. Within a few minutes he found himself dropping onto the balcony beside her. "You've done this before," he said.

She nodded and inspected the panes in the window. Just the fact they were of glass told Kormak that Scar's operation was making money. In the west only the richest could afford glass. City councils often taxed people based on the number of glass windows they had. It was as good an indicator of wealth as any other. She produced a very narrow, very thin dagger and worked it slowly into the window frame; softly and slowly she sawed away and the lowest pane began to slide out. It fell quietly backwards and made a gap. She put her hand through behind the next highest pane and repeated the procedure catching the glass before it could fall as the small pane toppled backwards. After a couple of minutes she reached the latch and undid it, and opened the window.

She crawled through and gestured for Kormak to follow. They were in a quiet chamber, lit by moonlight. Nuala moved over to the doorway and opened it. Kormak followed her. They were looking out into a long corridor, lined with doorways.

"Scar uses these rooms for his wealthier clients. The ones with the lighted windows will be occupied by some of the local gentry, puffing away on his wares."

"Nice to know," said Kormak, "but that's not going to help us find Razhak."

"You think it will still be wearing Ana's body," she asked.

"It most likely is. I doubt it would want even Scar to see it shift forms. That would be likely to turn even an orc against it."

"What if it has? Could you still spot it?"

"There are signs, if you know what to look for."

"It might be helpful to know what those are."

"I don't have the time to lecture you on the subject," Kormak said. "Stick close to me and I will let you know if we are in his presence."

She nodded. They pushed on along the corridor and came to a flight of stairs leading down. A man and a scantily clad woman came up them and Kormak realised they had their own business. Nuala pushed herself against him as she had done when the guard appeared earlier and he hoped the bar-girl and her client did not look too closely at them.

"The girls use the private rooms upstairs," she said, after they separated. She seemed to be breathing a little faster than normal. Kormak knew he was. "There's supposed to be other rooms in the basement, with chains and other more exotic devices for those who like such things."

"Scar has his finger in a lot of different businesses," Kormak said.

"This Vandemar, big man," she said. "People do what they have to."

They continued down the stair and came out on the balcony overlooking the common room. It had been tidied up since the fight earlier and was just as busy as it had been back then. Kormak stood in the shadows on the balcony and scanned the room, looking for any signs of Razhak.

"You planning on searching every room in this place?" Nuala asked.

"No," said Kormak, moving towards the door of the chamber from which Scar had emerged earlier. "I am going to ask for directions."

He pushed the door open and entered blade in hand. Ana was there, so was Scar and half a dozen other men. Nuala hung back, staying out of line of sight.

Seeing Ana Kormak sprang. Quick as he was Scar somehow got between them and parried his strike with his blades. Steel rang on steel.

"I was wondering when you would show up," Scar said. His voice was soft but his words carried. He struck at Kormak swift as a serpent. Kormak barely had time to parry.

"Do you know what you are doing? Who you are protecting?" Kormak asked. He countered swiftly, bringing his blade sweeping down towards Scar's face. Scar sprang backwards.

"Yes," said Scar. "It matters not to me if it preys on your weak race. I will have your heart and your blade and a life of endless challenge when your brethren come to seek it. I was First Blade of the Red Horde, taught Edge Rites by the Wolf Shamans. I will devour your brethren and absorb their prowess."

Kormak cursed quietly. The orc was serious. He believed he could ingest part of an enemy's prowess with his flesh and he welcomed the possibility of endless conflict with Kormak's order and a heroic death in battle. It was how orcs lived and how they wanted to die.

Scar struck. His blades were flickering lightning, dancing everywhere with dizzying speed. Kormak fell back towards the door, parrying, looking for an opening. Scar was not even breathing hard.

Kormak saw an opening. He knocked Scar's blade aside and stabbed his dwarf-forged sword into the orc's heart. Scar twisted, turning sideways. The blade passed through his side but not fatally. It had been a feint of a most daring and bloody kind.

Scar's massive hand reached out and he caught the Elder Sign hanging by its chain around Kormak's neck. It snapped and the sign went skittering free across the floor.

Before he could withdraw his blade, Razhak struck. He darted forward and stabbed out with his hand. Pain spasmed through Kormak and for a moment he lost control of his limbs. While he thrashed, two of Scar's men raced forward. Bludgeons slammed into Kormak's head. He fell to the floor, twisting to tell Nuala to get away. He need not have bothered. The girl was already gone.

Kormak awoke feeling bruised and chilled. Metal chains restrained his limbs and chilled him where they touched flesh. He looked up and saw Ana. Rotten skin had sloughed away from her flesh now. An eerie green glow glittered within her eyes. Looking around Kormak saw frightened thugs looking at her in horror. Behind her was Scar repairing the links of the chain of Kormak's damaged Elder Sign. The orc's wounded side was bound. Seeing Kormak awake, he showed his fangs, put down the amulet and picked up his blades.

Kormak realised his mail shirt had been removed and his amulets. His blade lay on a table in the far corner of the room. He had been stripped of all protection, physical and spiritual, and he doubted his life had been spared for any good reason.

"I had to use up most of my energy with that last spell," said Razhak. "It ruined this body, took the life from it. I need a new form so

I have patched yours up. It is magnificent, a shell that should house me till I reach Tanyth."

"Kill me and my order will send two more to hunt you."

A soft, corrupt phlegmy laugh emerged from the possessed woman's throat. "I have heard enough about your order. I shall leave the blade here with my friend Scar and I shall disappear. They can reclaim the sword. That is all they care about."

Kormak felt the touch of the Ghul. It was chill and clammy. Ana's hand felt oddly sticky as if some small vampiric creeper was attaching itself to his breast. A coldness radiated out from the point of contact, sending tendrils burrowing deep into Kormak's chest, through his veins and up his spine. At first it was not painful, not even unpleasant, only faintly disturbing.

He looked up into Ana's face. The possessed woman's face glowed from within. Her flesh was starting to turn black and liquefy. A reddish glow burned in her eyes, growing brighter with every passing heartbeat. Through Ana's stolen eyes, something ageless watched him, her lips twisted into a smile as the skin ran like wax from a melting candle.

Suddenly, Kormak felt as if a thousand needles stabbed into his flesh where the cold hand rested above his heart. The chill spread suddenly and searingly, so cold it burned, along all those lines of power. His whole body spasmed as his muscles reacted. His fingers opened and closed and they did not do so at his command, nor at the command of anyone else . . . yet.

He felt in some way like a puppet at the end of a string and at the same time could feel an ominous sense of presence growing in his mind, as in some dreadful dream. It was as if some dark and awful monster, lurking out of sight, was coming ever closer.

His heart raced. His mouth went dry. He felt dizzy and if it was not for the chains, he would not have been able to stand up right. He felt as if he was falling into a black pit that yawned at his feet, an endless, empty chasm in which he would never hit bottom.

His limbs thrashed. He bit on his tongue. He felt a tearing sensation as if his spirit was being ripped free of his body and something else was trying to elbow it aside and take its place within the house of his flesh.

Images started to flicker into his mind. Bubbling up like old memories suddenly remembered. Some of them belonged to him and some of them belonged to someone else. He felt tendrils of alien thought riffle through his mind, like a burglar looking through the possessions found in a trunk. He felt an eager, gloating presence, keen to take possession of all of them, of every little thing he remembered.

He saw a village in the mountains of Aquilea, everyone dead, corpses sprawling in the muddy streets, as cold as the fingers that touched his chest, dead eyes staring at the sky, mouths open in prayer to a god that never answered. He saw an eight year old boy standing in the ruins of a smithy, clutching his father's hammer, confronting an evil as old as the world while that evil watched him with mocking eyes. The ancient being walked over to the boy and took away the hammer, and it reached out and touched his cheek. You I will spare to take word to the world but one day, child, when you least expect it, I will come for you again. On that day, you will die!

He felt Razhak's sense of shock in the invading presence. It realised what it was seeing. It was looking on something coeval with itself, a thing that had once been its master, a Lord of the Old Ones, a renegade outside the Law.

Kormak took advantage of its surprise to strike back, as he had been taught by the masters of Mount Aethelas long ago. He threw all of his willpower into envisioning an Elder Sign in his mind. The Ghul recoiled from him, leaving him with a fragment of its memories. Of a world before the coming of men, of ancient beings who had once served the Old Ones and who sought to emulate them.

He watched the Sunlanders arrive borne on the wings of storm from their sinking island continent to claim the lands of the Old Ones in the name of their brilliant, solar god. He saw the Ghul take advantage of the war to rebel against their masters.

He saw Tanyth, a gigantic city with a dome of magic over it and towers whose minarets glowed like the moon as lightning danced from spire to spire. He saw the things that looked somewhat like men, but were not, lie down in sarcophagi and have their essence strengthened until they could exist outside the housing of flesh. He felt a sense of triumph. They had emulated their masters. They were immortal.

The Ghul struck back at him. A wave of power rushed inwards battering at the walls he had created around his self with the Elder Sign. It smashed through them and dug its talons into his soul and began to shake lose his memories once more. He saw that eight year old boy still standing in the ruins of an empty village. The ancient evil was gone, as inexplicably as it had come, leaving him alone in the place of death. He heard the sound of a horse. He looked up and he saw a grim-faced man ride in, with a dwarf-forged sword slung on his back. The man looked wary at the sight but he did not look afraid. He dismounted and moved towards the boy suspiciously, as if he thought the child might be a demon wearing a different form.

The boy stood watching, clutching his father's hammer. The man reached out and touched him with an amulet, which did not burn and then asked him what had happened.

Kormak saw that Razhak was beginning to understand. Taking advantage of the demon's confusion, he countered. The memories came in a tide of images, intermingling as the two spirits fought for possession of his body. Kormak was not going to give up. The tide of memories brought back fresh recollections of his training in how to resist magical influence. He strengthened his wards, clawed back at Razhak.

Images flickered through his mind. The bodiless Ghuls raced around the world, disembodied immortal creatures that yet had the appetites born of flesh and which now hungered for the experiences they could no longer have. Disquieting tidings came, as Ghuls started to flicker and fade. There was a flaw in their magic. They had not become as independent of the flesh as they had thought. They could still die, coming apart in a welter of entropic energy, losing form and coherence, as if there was nothing to anchor them to reality.

More memories were ripped from Kormak's mind. He saw the boy and the Guardian approach the towering spire of Mount Aethelas. He caught sight of the ancient fortress-monastery for the first time. He saw himself placed with the other novices. Once again he picked up a training sword and surprised the masters with how good he was with it. He recalled the long years of training and learning. He saw himself grow to become a hulking youth with quick reflexes and a quicker temper, a black-haired cuckoo among the golden-haired second offspring of the Sunlander nobility from whom the vast majority of Guardians were drawn.

He saw the first desperate attempts of the Ghuls to find out what had gone wrong. Without their physical forms it was difficult to work the magical engines they had thought they had no more need for. He saw the Ghuls learn how to seize the forms of others, starting with beasts and working their way up to sentients.

Humans proved best. They lacked the spiritual protections of the Old Ones and there were so many of them, scattering so far and so fast across the lands that the weakest could be picked off without the Ghuls being noticed. Some acquired herds of humans, with scores of new bodies to be taken possession of. Some set themselves up as kings. Some led human armies against their former masters, the Old Ones. Some were worshipped as Gods just as the Old Ones had been. They returned to Tanyth and made a home there, with herds of subject humans to worship and guard them. Life was good until the Emperor Solareon intervened to free the humans from their worship of false gods. His armies smashed Tanyth, bound the Ghuls in great amphorae with potent spells, questioned them as to their secrets, then one day he rode away to make war on new enemies, never to return. His successor, fanatical with holy rage, threw the amphorae into the darkest part of the World Ocean, to rest in the darkness of the ocean floor for long cold millennia. Kormak was struck by a vast sense of cosmic loneliness. Razhak had encountered none of his own kind for centuries. It was possible he was the last.

He saw flashes from his own life again as Razhak struggled back. He saw his apprenticeship to Master Malan and the long hunt that had led to him being awarded his blade. He saw the orc wars of his youth when he had saved the life of King Brand and slaughtered orc chieftains, reaping lives like wheat. He saw himself travel through deserts of ash where the dead men walked, and confronting witches and wizards and Old Ones and demons. He saw the point where his path crossed with Razhak's and the long hunt across the wastelands had begun.

He sensed now the Ghul's fear as it desperately tried to elude its implacable pursuer and its growing despair as he eluded every trap, overcame every spell, sought out every refuge. He felt a gnawing sense of terror as the demon realised it could not escape and would have to turn at bay. He felt at last a flow of direct contact between himself and Razhak.

Why have you pursued me, Man? Why have you bedevilled my footsteps for so long?

Because I must. You have broken the Law. You have slain and maimed and killed. You must be stopped.

I merely do what I must to stay alive. As you do to cattle, as wolves do to deer.

We are not cattle. We live and think and feel. You have no right to slay us.

Your sheep would say the same to you, if they could but speak.

But they cannot and we can and that is the difference. You seek to live. We seek to live. In the end all things must die.

You would not if you allow me to take your form. Part of you would live forever with the multitudes inside of me.

That is not what I seek.

No. You seek death. Even as you bring it.

You project your own desires on to me. As I would to you. In the end there is no escape for either of us.

If you have your way and kill me your world will be poorer. All that I have seen and been and done, all my memories and dreams, all that remains of a people will be gone.

It is the same for all of us. With every man's death, a world disappears.

I have fought Death so long. I will not let it end like this.

Kormak sensed the demon gathering what remained of its strength for a final strike at him. A surge of agony and memory swept over him. He resisted the onrushing wave like a boulder resisting the tide, letting it break around him against the hard rock of his will until the moment was passed and Razhak was gone, leaving him feeling strangely alone.

A loud crash sounded. Kormak opened his eyes and saw the doors to the torture cell were open. Guards poured down the stair. Nuala was with them. Scar moved to block their way.

The Ghul raised its hands and chanted a spell, a wave of energy flowed out from it, stunning the newcomers and the orc and his followers alike. It would have overcome Kormak too had he not been prepared by his spiritual conflict with Razhak to resist it.

The effort of that last spell proved too much for Razhak. Ana's body was coming apart, decomposing into horrible black fluid, skin bursting and putrefying even as Kormak watched. The darkly shimmering form of the Ghul emerged and flickered around. Tendrils of light touched Scar and he screamed. A moment later his eyes glowed and Kormak knew that the Ghul had claimed another victim.

It turned to look at him for a moment and there was something there, some flicker of sympathy perhaps, or at least of shared understanding. The orc's fangs drew back in rage and Kormak knew that the Ghul was going to come for him. He leaned back against the wall, giving the chains some slack. If the Ghul came within reach he would try and smash it down with the bunched links of metal. The Ghul shook its head as if reading his resolution. It reeled up the stairs and away.

Kormak's muscles ached, his bones felt as if their marrow was molten. His brain felt empty as if much of what he was had been lost, and he realised it was merely the absence of the gigantic presence that Razhak had been. He strained with all his might against the chains. They had never been intended to resist a man as strong as he. They came away from the walls, leaving him free to stagger over to the board of keys pinned against the walls and find the one that would free him.

He walked over to where his sword lay, picked it up and strapped it on. He took his amulets and his armour and put them on too. Nuala stirred faintly. It seemed she was still alive. He walked over to her and touched her with his Elder Sign, hoping it might disrupt any inimical energy that remained in her form. Her eyes opened and she looked up at him.

"You owe me," she said.

"For bringing the guard?" he asked, as he helped her to her feet.

"I told them you were here. It was the fastest way of getting them to come. Maybe the only way to get them to break into Scar's place."

"You did well," he said.

She looked at the recumbent form of the guards. "Will they be all right?"

"If you are, they will be. And I think I had best be gone when they awake. It will be easier than explaining."

She nodded. "You'd better find, Darien. You owe him money."

"What do I owe you?" She reached up and stroked his cheek.

"I am sure we can work out some method of payment that is satisfactory for both of us," she said.

They stumbled up the stairs and out into the deserted tavern. Outside the open door, the night waited. Somewhere out there, Razhak was running for his life. Kormak knew where he was going now with utter certainty. He would find the demon in the ruins of Tanyth.

Death waited there for one of them. Tonight he did not care. He had debts to pay in the here and now.

THAT WAY LIES DEATH

"THAT WAY LIES death," said the old man. The frown deepened the lines on his leathery face into trenches. A mad gleam shone in his eye. Perhaps it was the look of ascetic fanaticism brought on by too much exposure to the desert sun or possibly he truly had been touched by holiness. Why else would he be sitting half-naked by a milestone in the desert along the ancient road to Sunhaven?

Kormak looked in the direction the hermit had indicated with his wizened hand. It did not look any different from the rest of the wastes the road passed through. It was a harsh dry land where the only touch of colour came from the yellowish blooms of some hardy creosote plants.

Kormak removed his helmet and wiped the sweat from his forehead. He was hot and all too aware of it. His leather tunic and mail shirt had not been intended for a climate like this. Again he considered removing them and putting them with the cloak in his saddlebags but the road to Sunhaven was famous for its bandits and its monsters and he had no desire to die with an arrow through him if it could be avoided. At the moment, he thought sourly. Another few hours of this and he might feel differently.

"Death seems to be everywhere here," said Kormak. "This would be an easy place for a man to leave this life."

"In yonder direction lies the lost city of Tanyth," the old man said. "It is guarded by demons, the haunt of the damned. They fly over the desert in a night when it would take men a week's ride or more to get here."

Kormak looked at him again. "You have chosen a strange place to dwell then."

The old man smiled and gestured in the direction of the nearby hills. "I have my cave. I have my spring. I have retreated from the wickedness of the cities of Men. I contemplate the mysteries of the Holy Sun here where the sky is clear and His light is brightest. I do not fear demons for He watches over me."

"What sort of demons are there?" Kormak asked. He had a professional interest in such things.

"Lamia, succubae, she-fiends. They visit me in the night. Disport themselves lewdly. Seek to tempt me back to the ways of flesh. I reject them."

Kormak wondered whether the Holy Sun was the only thing this ancient saw visions of and how real these temptations were. Perhaps they were simply projections of the desires the old man thought he had left behind. Perhaps not. Kormak had encountered too many demons to discount the possibility that the old man was right.

Kormak tapped the blade that hung over his shoulder. "I do not fear demons," he said.

"Ah but you are a Guardian of the Order of the Dawn. I know your kind. One passed through the City of Light in the years of my youth. Many men died before he departed. Once he was gone, the killings ceased." He let the words and their accusation hang in the air, all the while keeping his bright, mad gaze focused directly on Kormak.

"Such is often the way," Kormak said. The old man rubbed his grey stubble.

"They say the men who died were wicked. No doubt some of them were. Others were not. I am not sure your order is as righteous as it claims."

Kormak agreed but it did not seem politic to say so. The old man's gaze shifted and he focused his eyes back on the road. Riders were approaching. Pennons fluttered on the end of their lances. They held the short moon-curved bow so common in this land. When they got closer, he would doubtless find they were armed with scimitars.

"Riders often pass along this road. Some of them are charitable," said the old hermit. Kormak fumbled some change from his purse and dropped it in front of the old man. He laughed and picked it up then rose to his feet and handed it back to Kormak

"I have no use for silver out here. It would only tempt men of violence and make me think of the foul uses I could put it to back in the city."

Kormak shrugged. "I cannot spare food or water; I have a long journey ahead of me."

"Perhaps I can spare you some then," said the old man. "Water at least. This road is no place to be caught without water."

The riders were close enough now that Kormak could see he was wrong. They carried the straight blades of Sunlander Templars. Their gear was an odd mix of light armour, recurved lunar bows and western helmets and swords. Kormak guessed these were descendants of the Oathsworn who had set out to reclaim the Sacred Lands from the moondogs generations ago. They had adapted to the local climate. There were obviously some things he could learn from them.

One of the men was as richly dressed as a prince. His robes were silk, his breastplate worked with intricate shapes that were only vaguely recognisable as Elder Signs. The patterns were almost lost as if the people who had made the device were more concerned with decoration than protection from the Old Ones and the Shadow. The rest of the men were warriors, either feudal retainers or well-paid mercenaries. They had a hard competent look to them. Kormak took his place beside the old man. He did not really expect violence here but you never knew. The normal laws of men were sometimes suspended in the wastelands.

The lead rider came closer. Kormak could see he was a handsome young man with very dark hair and very white teeth. His hair fell in ringlets to his shoulders. His beard was well-trimmed to two points. He looked foppish but there was something about the way he sat in the saddle and assessed Kormak's stance that told the Guardian he was not quite as soft as he looked.

"I see another has come to consult you, father," the newcomer said. There was something taunting in his speech and at the same time something deferential. There was respect there as well as mockery as if the youth sought to prove how cynical he was and yet at the same time, in his heart of hearts, feared the wrath of the old man's god. It was an attitude Kormak had seen many times among the spoiled nobility of the far west. The young man looked at Kormak. "Not a Sunlander and not an easterner either. That is a puzzle."

"An Aquilean," Kormak said. "It's north-west of Taurea."

"You are a long way from home."

"Sir Kormak is on a quest, my son." There was something odd in the way the hermit said those words as well. "He is hunting a demon."

"Then that is a dwarf-forged blade upon his shoulder. Interesting. I had not expected ever to see such a thing. Would you mind if I took a look at it?" He held out his hand in complete expectation that Kormak would simply hand the blade over.

"Yes," Kormak said. "I would."

His tone obviously rankled the retainers. They reached for their weapons.

"Tell your men I can kill you before they reach me, and then I will kill them," Kormak said. He said it loudly enough so that the youth did not need to.

"Are you really so good with the blade?" the youth asked. He did not seem in the least bit frightened.

"Yes," Kormak said. "But if you feel the need to put that to the test, by all means, go ahead."

The youth smiled. "That will not be necessary. It was rude of me to ask a Guardian to part with his weapon. I spoke without thinking. There is no harm done to my dignity. I hope you will accept my apology, Sir Kormak."

The retainers at once relaxed their grips on their sword hilts. They did not look any less wary though. All of them inspected Kormak with fierce, hawk-like eyes.

"The matter is forgotten," said Kormak.

"Very good. Let us start again. I am Prince Luther Na Veris of the city of Sunhaven. I have come here today to bring alms to this noble and long-suffering hermit," Again there was that faint and ironic emphasis in this speech, "and then I will ride back to the city. I hope you will do me the honour of riding a ways with me and perhaps guesting in my mansion."

"I would be honoured to ride with you, Prince, but I am on a most urgent mission and I cannot accept your hospitality."

"You can tell me of your quest as we ride. Perhaps I may help you in some way. I am not without influence in these parts and it will do my soul some good to aid the righteous."

There was still an element of mockery in Luther's words, just as there had been when he spoke to the hermit, but Kormak sensed the underlying seriousness of the young man's intent. "That would be a blessing."

The Prince nodded and then gestured and two of them men at arms dismounted and took leather-bound packages from their saddlebags. They brought them to the hermit, set them down beside him with respectful bows and then retreated back to their steeds.

The Prince walked over to the hermit and they exchanged murmured words. There seemed to be some quiet debate going on, possibly of a religious nature. Kormak studied the guards as they waited. They looked back at him. Most of them were indifferent but some glared. They had taken his earlier words as a challenge and they were keen to show that they were not afraid.

In the clear sky above the desert Kormak saw a hawk in flight. As he watched it stooped, and he knew that somewhere in the distance death had touched the desert.

A moment later Prince Luther returned. "With your permission, Sir Guardian, let us be away!"

They rode side by side towards the city, with the line of retainers stretching out behind them. Kormak was uncomfortably aware that there were men with bows at his back and that he might be shot without warning. The die was cast though, and he did not believe any of the retainers would attack him without a word from the Prince. He paid very close attention to Luther Na Veris as they rode.

A warm wind had sprung up from the desert. It made Kormak's eyes feel dry and the skin of his face itch. The Prince produced a scarf and drew it across the bottom half of his face. The warriors did likewise, gratefully. Kormak realised that they would not do the thing until Luther did.

The Prince gazed at Kormak sidelong. "It is strange for a Guardian to be so far from Mount Aethelas."

"I hunt a demon. I have tracked it for hundreds of leagues, from Vandemar and beyond. I think my hunt will come to an end soon."

"A demon? Of what sort?" The question was casually put, in the same way as a wizard might put it.

"You are a sorcerer?" Kormak asked. The Prince laughed.

"No. I am a dabbler. I have read some grimoires and some ancient texts written by the Old Ones. I read them more for the imagery than the knowledge. I find it helps with my compositions."

"You are a scholar then."

"Of sorts. It is my poor pretence to be a poet."

"Luther of Sunhaven," said Kormak.

"You know my name I see. It is flattering to be renowned as far away as the cold hills of Aquilea."

"I heard your name at the Court of the King of Taurea. A bard had set certain of your lyrics to music."

"I wrote a cycle of love poems in my salad days. They enjoyed a certain ephemeral popularity. They are still sung in taverns and sailors carry songs far."

"I had not realised you were a prince."

"It is a not uncommon title in the Sacred Lands," Luther said. "A lot of nobles awarded themselves high honours when they stole these lands from the Seleneans. I am descended from one. There are many others. Princes are as common in Sunhaven as knights in Taurea or so they say." He smiled affably. "But you were telling me of your quest. It is not every day I get to meet a man who hunts demons." Once again there was an element of irony in the Prince's speech, mocking and undercutting his protestations of interest.

"It's not every day I meet a Prince who is also a poet."

"I assure you I have had by far the less interesting life of the two of us."

The walls of the city appeared on the horizon. They were massive. Sunhaven had quite clearly been built to withstand a siege. The walls extended outwards in buttressed points. They were ten times the height of a man and Kormak had heard it said you could drive a chariot along the top of them. Over the walls a gigantic white tower worked with patterns of gold loomed over the city, dominating the entire skyline.

"It is true," Kormak said. "The walls of Sunhaven are laid out in the same pattern as the Elder Sign."

Luther nodded. "The walls of all five of the Holy Cities are. It is said that if you looked down from the sky, the way the Holy Sun does, that the roads between them would form the pattern of a gigantic Elder Sign as well. It may be true. These ancient roads run straight enough."

"Is that so?"

"It makes you wonder, doesn't it? How the ancients did it. Built so straight and so far that they could enclose an entire kingdom within the Elder Sign's sacred protection."

"Some would say they were inspired by the Sun himself. After all it was one of the Prophets who commanded the work."

Luther smiled indulgently. "Personally I wonder why they did it. Elder Signs are used to keep demons in as well as out."

"You think this land is some sort of prison?"

"There are certain old grimoires that hint as much."

"Go on."

"Some say this land is a massive gateway to the Realms of Shadow, that armies of demons lie in wait beneath the crust of reality to emerge and work evil. They say it is from this place that the Shadow first entered the world, before the coming of Men. That is why the Holy Cities were built here—they are watchtowers against another onslaught by the Shadow."

"There are regions where such things happen," Kormak said. "But I have never encountered one so huge."

"But you have visited such places?"

Kormak nodded.

"We really should talk you and I. There are many things I would question you about."

"Would that I had the time, Prince." Luther nodded affably at this refusal. He did not seem at all troubled by the response.

"It is a strange thought, is it not, that the earth upon which we walk may have the legions of Shadow beneath it?"

"It is a disturbing thought."

"This can be a disturbing land."

"But one that can inspire a poet," Kormak said. "If his imagination ran in certain directions."

"I hear a hint of the Inquisition in your voice, Sir Kormak, the trace of fanatical disapproval."

"It was an observation, that was all."

"I have noticed that certain of your observations sound like threats."

"I would say that perception lay within the mind of the listener. In this case, at least."

"You debate like a priest, sir."

"I was taught by them," Kormak admitted.

"That in no way surprises me," said the Prince. He shaded his eyes with his hand and stared off into the distance. "I think we shall be in time," he said.

The city came ever closer. Kormak could see that many buildings lay outside the huge walls and were dwarfed by them. It was often the case in this world he had found. Cities outgrew their ancient defences. In the west there were places where the walls marked the age of certain parts of cities the way the rings of a tree did.

There was no real boundary between the desert and the outer city. At first they merely rode between isolated white-washed mud-brick houses, which became more and more common until they were ragged, half-empty streets and then densely packed ones. People went from being relatively rare on the outskirts to swarming crowds as they got closer to the walls.

Soon they were surrounded by hawkers and water-sellers and jugglers and clowns. Beggars and thieves moved closer as well. About half of the folk were dressed in western style tunics and britches made from light linen fabrics. The others, darker skinned, were garbed in flowing robes of the Desert Tribes. The men in britches tended to wear the Sign of the Sun and walk proudly and aggressively. The desert men wore Lunar symbols and spoke softly.

Prince Luther nodded to one of his men, the same one as had given the package to the hermit and the man produced a purse and tossed a shower of small coins into the crowd. People scrambled to pick them up as the Prince rode through.

Ahead of them a gate surmounted by an Elder Sign loomed ten spans high. It had huge valves of bronze. Armoured men stood on either side. Prince Luther studied the sky. It was starting to get dark. "Good," he said. "The North Gate is still open. There will be no need to spend time in some Low City Tavern and wait for the dawn."

"I regret I must take my leave of you, Prince," said Kormak. "And seek a bed for the night."

"It would do me great honour if you accepted my hospitality, Guardian. You will lose no time or money and more importantly you will not get your throat slit in some low dive. It does happen here."

"Men have tried to cut my throat before, Prince. I am still here."

"I have a library containing many volumes that might interest you. I have scrolls concerning the Ghul and their city in which you might find knowledge valuable on your quest. I have maps too. I am quite the collector in my way."

Kormak glanced at him sidelong. In that moment he was reminded a little of Lord Tomas who had freed Razhak originally. Luther had a similar intensity. Still the things he offered might prove useful. "That would indeed be useful."

"Then it is settled. You will accompany me to my mansion and you can consult with my library and I will avail myself of the opportunity to pick your brain of knowledge and bore you with displays of my own erudition."

"Very well, Prince Luther, I accept your offer. For this night alone."

"Capital." They rode through the North Gate. It was like riding into a tunnel, dark and shadowy. It was full of men with donkeys and camels and carts all trying to get passed the guards. Prince Luther was obviously recognised for he was waved through as were all those with him.

The streets of the Old City were very different from those of the new. They were laid out in perfectly straight lines and all of the buildings showed a similarity of architecture, a symmetry of proportion, that marked them as having been built at the same time, in a different age of the world.

"Laid out according to the geomantic principles of the ancient Solari," said Luther, when he noticed Kormak's glance. "They built this city in the First Age of Men when the power of the Empire was at its height."

All of the streets led to a gigantic citadel whose single central tower rose like a spear aimed at the sky. At first glance the buildings were as impressive as all the work of the ancients but when he looked closer he could see everything had been repaired in a patchwork fashion, that many of the mansions were crumbling, that smaller buildings and newer had sprung up between the older ones.

"The city was not always in the hands of the Sunlanders," Luther said. Once again it was as if he was reading Kormak's thoughts. "There were centuries of neglect while the Seleneans held Sunhaven. They did so until the Oathsworn reclaimed the Tower of the Sun. Some say it is only a matter of time before they do again. Our hold on this land is still quite precarious. Without aid from the West we can hold out for a generation at most."

"The Kingdoms of the West have their own problems," Kormak said. "They are not united as they were in the Time of the Oathswearing."

"The same problem could be said to exist here," the Prince said. "There are those who think we should come to an accommodation with the moon-worshippers. Others think we should withdraw before we are over-run."

"What do you think?" Kormak asked.

"I believe it is inevitable that the city will fall back into the hands of the Seleneans. This is an isolated pocket of Solar worship now. We are surrounded on all sides by lands that are either debated or have been swamped by the moondogs."

They rode into a wide avenue of walled mansions, all with a clear view of the tower. It was clear they had been spotted for servants were already opening the gates of Prince Luther's mansion while guards watched from the flanking towers. As they rode into the courtyard it occurred to Kormak that every wealthy man's house in the city must be a small self-contained fortress.

Now he was trapped within one.

A fountain stood in the courtyard. Solar angels held great amphora above their heads and from them poured water. Orange trees stood in small enclosed walled gardens. Servants came forward to take the horses. Kormak allowed his to be led to the stable.

A majordomo advanced on Prince Luther, bowed and presented him with some scrolls. The Prince broke their seals casually and read them as they walked into the cool interior of the building. A halo of servants trailed them as well as the two bodyguards who had disbursed the Prince's money to the crowd. The rest of them seemed to have taken entry into the house as a signal that they were dismissed. Clearly there was a routine to this place and everyone knew their part in it.

Luther strolled through corridors lined with beautiful statues and entered a low courtyard opened to the sky. There was seating all around it. On a chair at its edge, a woman sat, reading a book.

"Sister," Luther said. "We have a guest."

The woman looked up and assessed Kormak with a cool gaze. There was a definite family resemblance to the Prince. They had the same dark curly hair, very white teeth and compelling dark eyes. She was very lovely. She put the book down on the table beside her, after marking her place with a silk ribbon.

She rose and made a courtly curtsey. Kormak responded with a formal bow. She placed her hand over her heart. "Welcome to our home, Guardian of the Dawn."

"Olivia is the scholar of the family," Luther said. "She has studied art, philosophy, history and alchemy. She understood the significance of the way you wear your blade as soon as she saw it."

"You are a long way from Mount Aethelas," the woman said.

"Sir Kormak is on a quest. He hunts a demon."

"There are no shortage of those in the Wastes beyond the Holy Road."

"He hunts one in particular, a Ghul."

"I thought those were all gone from the world. Imprisoned by Solareon or exterminated by your Order, Sir Guardian."

"There is one left," Kormak said. He felt like he was interrupting a conversation between these two. Prince Luther seemed happy to answer any questions his sister addressed to Kormak.

"But not for long if Sir Kormak has his way," Luther said. The woman sank back into her chair and with a graceful gesture indicated they should join her. She rang a bell, three times, with a particular rhythm. It must have been an accepted signal for in a short time a servant girl arrived with a silver tray containing apple tea for three. It was very sweet. Prince Luther added honey.

"How did you encounter, my brother, Sir Kormak?"

"He was talking to our father," said Luther before Kormak could reply. Kormak studied the Prince and his sister. He was trying to recall the old hermit's features. It was possible that there was a family resemblance there.

"I can see you have baffled the Guardian."

"The hermit is really your father?" Kormak said. "I thought you used the expression merely as a sign of respect."

"No! Our father has foresworn the world and its guilty pleasures. He has renounced all his estates and worldly goods and mistresses in favour of my sister and myself. He seeks to save his soul and redeem his sins."

"He has many sins to atone for," said Olivia. Luther shot her a warning glance. She shook her head almost imperceptibly as if she was telling her brother she would not be silenced.

"Our father was a famously wicked man, Sir Kormak," she said. "He studied for the priesthood when he was young and then abandoned the path when his elder brother died and he inherited the estate. It is said he broke all of his priestly vows in a single night that they still talk about down in the Street of Seven Pleasures."

"I have heard of novices who did the same," Kormak said.

"From your own order?" Luther sounded curious.

"My order does not ask men to foreswear pleasures of the flesh."

"Save for one," Olivia said. "You may not marry."

"That hardly means foreswearing women, sister. You are not so innocent!"

Olivia smiled. She did not look embarrassed. She considered Kormak in a measuring way and then looked back at her brother.

"Father insists on his folly then," Olivia said. "He will not return and let us care for him."

"It is hardly folly to embrace godliness," Luther said.

"Is that what he is doing?" Olivia said. "I thought this was just a new form of egotism. He is enjoying the drama of renunciation. Once he is bored with it, he will return. Be certain of it."

"My sister is a cynic, Sir Kormak," said Luther. She inclined her head. Kormak decided it was not just the father who enjoyed drama in this family. They seemed happy to have an audience to play out their discussion in front of. He started to get the sense that for all the fact that they lived in the city these might be people isolated from normal society. Thinking of the bluff warriors he had encountered since he came to this land, Kormak had some idea how that might come about.

"She simply knows her father too well," said Olivia.

"I admit to the possibility of that," said Luther. The shadows were starting to lengthen. Servants appeared with lamps. They burned perfumed oil, not tallow. There was no shortage of money in the house.

"Tell me of your quest, Sir Kormak," said Olivia. "It has been centuries since any man has encountered a Ghul. They were rare even in these demon-haunted parts in this age of the world."

"That is strange is it not," said Kormak. "Tanyth was once their city."

"They ruled this land in the days between when they rebelled against the Old Ones and the coming of the Solarians," said Olivia.

"The First Empire broke them, destroyed Tanyth. The Emperor Solareon imprisoned the Ghul in punishment for their evil. Those who could fled from his wrath and were scattered over the world. Presumably there must have been some who were not in the city at all. There is considerable speculation on the subject among the ancient scholars."

"Razhak was in the city. He was imprisoned by Solareon. I handled the flask in which he was bound myself."

"Razhak," she said. "That is an evil name. He was a mighty wizard among the Ghul or so the old books claim."

"I can believe that. I saw as much in his mind when he tried to possess me."

The girl shuddered. Prince Luther looked quizzical. He tilted his head to one side. "Tried to possess you?"

"He failed," Kormak said, his tone making it clear he had no wish to discuss the matter further.

"And still you pursue the creature," said Olivia.

"I have followed this demon a long way. He has eluded me so far but soon the chase will end."

"How can you know that?" Luther asked.

"He is weakened and must return to Tanyth to use the great spell-engines there or he will die. Perhaps that is the wrong word. He will unravel. His life force is woven into a pattern of energy that should be self-sustaining."

Olivia looked up sharply. "But some part of it is undone and it is starting to unravel like a tapestry from which threads have been pulled."

"Exactly so." Kormak said.

The woman looked excited. "That confirms what Eraclius of Anacreon claimed," she said.

"It may be," said Kormak. "But I have not read any of that sage's works."

"We have a collection in our library," said Olivia. "You may study them before you retire. Of course, they are written in High Solari."

"I am familiar with the tongue," said Kormak.

"A Guardian would be," she said. "I am surprised you have not read Eraclius. I had always heard that the Library at Aethelas was the best in the world."

"It is lady, but I have read only a tiny fraction of its volumes. My duties are of a more active than scholarly nature."

"Of course," she said. "They would be. I will see to it that you are brought a selection of the scrolls pertaining to your quest. The knowledge they contain may prove useful to you."

"Thank you, Lady Olivia."

The Prince said, "We should eat now and I would question Sir Kormak about his career. There is a lot he can tell me and I would get it down while I have the chance."

Luther seemed as keen about this as his sister did about her scholarship. They were an odd couple with strange enthusiasms and a languor about them that seemed to fit their surroundings.

He began to suspect that they were perhaps more typical of the Sunlander aristocracy in this land than he had at first thought. There was a doomed quality about them, as if they were simply passing through this land, shadows in the light of the harsh sun, destined to vanish with the coming of night.

A servant brought in parchment and quills and Luther rose and sat himself at table. He began to ask Kormak about his life and his training and his travels. He was interested in the oddest things. Was he afraid when he confronted his first demon? What did it feel like to kill an immortal? Did he sometimes find himself sympathising with those he killed?

The last question obviously had a resonance with Luther. He clearly identified with the ancient immortals whose lives were being extinguished by one whose lifespan was an eyeblink to them. He wondered about the lost knowledge and what those eyes might have looked on. Certainly far more than Kormak would ever see no matter how far he travelled.

It was late when the servant finally showed Kormak to his chamber, illuminating the way with a lantern. The room was as luxuriously furnished as the rest of the mansion. A large four-poster bed in the western style was there, decorated with carvings in the ornate local fashion that were seemingly Elder Signs intended to ward the sleeper as they dreamt but which were so ornate that Kormak doubted they would function as intended.

He stripped off his armour but made sure his scabbarded sword was within easy reach on the bedside table. He threw open the shutters and looked out into the night. The moon rose huge and strange over the towers and minarets of the city. The Tower of the Sun loomed gigantically over everything. At its peak something burned like the beacon in a lighthouse. Kormak remembered being able to see that light from leagues away across the desert. He thought about Taurea and the lands of the West he had left behind. It would be winter there now. It was winter here but it just did not feel like it. He was a long, long way from home and he felt it.

There was a gentle knock on the door. Kormak picked up his scabbard and walked over to the door, unbolting it. Olivia stood there. She carried a bunch of scrolls tied up with a ribbon. Her dress was lighter than the one she had worn downstairs, revealing her figure. Her hair was pinned up revealing her neck.

"I brought you the works of Eraclius I talked about," she said.

"It was not necessary for you to bring them yourself, my lady," Kormak said.

"It is my pleasure to do so, Guardian," she said. "Do you mind if I come in?"

For a moment Kormak was reminded of stories of Old Ones who could only cross thresholds when invited. He had seen this woman in daylight though and he thought he would know if it was an elder being wearing her shape.

"You may." She entered the room, closed the door and put the bar in place. They looked at each other across the length of the room. The bed was a looming presence between them. She swallowed and then smiled as composedly as she had done in the atrium downstairs.

"I hope my brother did not keep you talking too long," she said. "He does not get the opportunity to speak with a man like you very often."

"It is unusual for a Prince to be so interested in my work."

"He is not really a Prince and I am not really a Princess," she said. "In the west we would be minor nobles at best."

"You would be wealthy ones," Kormak said. "Not many of the nobles I have encountered live like this."

She walked over towards him. He was very aware of the swishing her nightdress made as she moved. She stood in front of him, offering him the scrolls submissively. The smile on her face was anything but submissive.

"Why are you here?" Kormak asked.

"Do you find it so hard to believe a woman might find you attractive?"

"Many women have," Kormak said. "As I am sure many men have found you beautiful."

"I do not encounter many men," she said.

"Why would that be?" Kormak asked.

"We are not popular with our neighbours or with the local nobility in general. My father is regarded as a degenerate, my brother an effete poet. Some of his verses are regarded as scandalous. Many think him mad and that madness runs in our family."

"Do you think so?"

She shook her head. "He has morbid interests. They stimulate his imagination. He is not mad though. He really is a poet. I think he is going to offer to accompany you to Tanyth."

"Why would he do that?"

She leaned so close he could feel her scented breath.

"He is curious and they say only madmen visit Tanyth, that the place is accursed. He wants to go to the place that all men are afraid of, and he wants to return and write about it and so win fame."

"He is already famous. I had heard his name in Taurea."

"He wants to be remembered, to make his name immortal. It's the only certain form of immortality men will ever have, is it not?"

Kormak reached out and touched her cheek, ever so gently. She shivered and then leaned her face against his callused sword hand. "And you do not want him to go?" Kormak asked.

"On the contrary, I want to go with you." Her eyes were very large and wide and innocent and Kormak found that he did not trust her in the slightest. It did not stop him wanting her though.

"Why?"

"We can talk about that later," she said, leaning forward and bringing her lips close to his. They parted slightly. He kissed her and then swept her up and carried her to the bed.

The Lady Olivia lay naked on the bed. Part of her body was in shadow but that just made the white flesh and the curves he could see all the more voluptuous. She stroked his cheek with one soft hand. Her nails were long and had tiny runes worked on them in dye.

"Why do you want to go to Tanyth?" Kormak asked. She smiled at him sardonically, teeth glittering in the dark,

"No compliments, Sir Kormak. You are not very gallant."

"I am not a gallant man," he said.

"No, you are not," she said. "Perhaps that is why you are attractive. You do not speak of honour or nobility. You are not a hypocrite."

Kormak studied her face in the darkness. She seemed serious. He smiled. She obviously did not know him well. "You are projecting what you want to see onto me," he said.

"Most men would not tell a lovesick girl that."

"You are not a girl and you are not lovesick. Let us not pretend otherwise."

"You do not think there is even the slightest possibility of that?"

"I am certain."

"You do not understand what life is like here then. It is not often I see a handsome man who interests me. It is not often I have the chance to break out of here."

"Is that what you want?" She sat up suddenly and reached out and took his chin, playfully twisting so that he had to look directly at her.

"To be a woman in this land is to be a prisoner. We may not go out unaccompanied lest the moon-worshippers ravish us. We may not do this. We may not do that."

"You do not seem to accept many limits."

"My situation is unusual. Within the walls of this house I am mistress. Outside of them I must go veiled. I must become invisible"

"And you wish to be seen."

"I am not so unlike my brother, Sir Kormak. I am a scholar. I will write upon this subject. I too wish to be remembered."

"I will remember you."

She smiled. "That is a start," she said, reaching over to kiss him again.

At breakfast next morning they sat like strangers. It was odd to rest in the chair and look at the woman sitting there so cool and collected and to remember the passion of the previous evening.

Prince Luther strode into the atrium, sat down at the table, picked up a sweetmeat and said, "I have been thinking about your quest, Sir Kormak. I would like to go with you."

"It will be dangerous, Prince Luther," Kormak said. His conversation with Olivia the previous evening had prepared him for this.

"That will only spice the dish," said Luther. "I have a hankering to see Tanyth, to look upon its ancient wonders."

"Why have you not done so before?" Kormak asked.

"Because those who go there go mad or never return. I think that if I go in the company of a Guardian, I may return to tell the tale."

"My quest is not to protect you, Prince. It is to slay Razhak and end his evil. He has killed a number of people since he was freed. I will see that he kills no more."

"Understood, Sir Kormak, but I could be of help to you. I can provide maps, guides, supplies, warriors, finance an expedition. It is not just demons you must worry about in the wastes. There are bandits and wild beasts and other dangers. If we go together you would not need to worry about such things. Nor would you need to worry about being granted permission to cross certain lands or go to certain places."

Kormak understood the veiled threat there. The Prince could no doubt make it difficult for him to leave the city if he wanted or place other obstacles in his path. And to tell the truth he could see certain advantages in taking up the Prince on his offer.

"Will your soldiers accompany you into Tanyth? You said that men fear the place."

"They can await us at a safe distance from the city. I do not fear to enter the city."

"Very well, I accept your offer," said Kormak. Olivia stared at him very hard. "On one condition . . . That your sister accompanies us as well."

The Prince glanced between Kormak and his sister. His smile was slow and a little sad. He clearly sensed that something had passed between them.

"So that's the way it is," Luther said. "Very well. I accept. All three of us will go to Tanyth."

He said it as a child might when considering a treat. Kormak wondered if Luther really knew what he was letting himself in for. He wondered if he knew what he was letting himself in for himself.

"We need to leave immediately," Kormak said. "We need to stop Razhak before he can find his spell-engines and perform his ritual."

It did not take Luther long to arrange things. His guards were well drilled and his stewards efficient. He was a wealthy man with little difficulty getting supplies. There were horses in his stables and mules. Watersacks were filled from the fountains and well. Maps were brought from the library. By noon, they were ready to go. A line of soldiers headed out with the Prince and his sister riding at the front with Kormak.

Olivia was dressed for travel in a cowled robe with a silk veil over her face. The veil was so thin as to be almost translucent and the effect was to hint at and accentuate her beauty rather than hide it. Much to his surprise she had a sword scabbarded at her waist and a bow on her saddle. On her belt were pouches for herbs and metal vials of alchemical substances held in leather loops.

Sensing the direction of his gaze, she said, "I wanted to learn as a child and my father saw no reason not to teach me. It was one of the advantages of having so unorthodox and disreputable a parent."

"My sister is actually very good with both weapons," said Prince Luther. "Better than many men."

"I shall take your word for it."

Kormak saw that they were being watched as they rode through the streets. It must have made an interesting procession for many people, the Prince and his retainers and a veiled and wealthy woman riding beside a Guardian, equipped for a long journey. Doubtless spies and newsmongers would be carrying the tale to all corners of the city within the hour. There would surely be people who would wonder what they were doing. Kormak did not care as long as it did not interfere with his mission.

He had a sense that events were coming to a close, that one way or another his hunt for Razhak would end in Tanyth. He pushed the thought to one side. In a hunt like this it was as well not to believe such feelings. He could take nothing for granted, not even the loyalty of the people he was with. They had their own agendas and he was not sure they were the ones they said they had.

One thing was certain, he would find out before the end.

The city receded behind them, the slums and hovels outside the walls gradually shrinking and vanishing until all that was visible were the gigantic walls, made pristine by distance and desert light. The Tower of the Sun loomed over them like the spear of a Titan thrust into the earth in the middle of the city.

They rode in silence, save for the whistle of the wind and the crunching of the friable ground under their horses' hooves. Prince Luther seemed happy. He smiled as if contemplating some pleasing secret. Olivia glanced around as if she had never seen desert before. Surely that could not be the truth of the matter, Kormak thought.

His mouth had an odd gritty taste in it and his throat always felt a little dry, as if thirst was an ever present demon waiting to strike. He found himself glancing around at the mules with their cargoes of supplies and checking the skins that dangled from his own saddle.

Olivia glanced over her shoulder too, gazing north and Kormak wondered if she was thinking of her father in his cave. It seemed odd, Kormak thought, that a man should give up the wealth that so many wanted in exchange for the poverty so many had. He had chosen to become a beggar when he had been a Prince.

No. That was not strictly speaking true. His children still visited him. They brought him small gifts. In a way they showed that they still cared and that there was a path back to what he had once been should he choose to take it. That was not the same as the poverty of the true poor, who had no choices. He understood what it was that

Olivia meant about her father. In his way he was still a rich man playing at being poor even if he chose to endure real discomfort.

Perhaps in the same way as, at this moment, his children were playing at being adventurers. Kormak was sure they understood the dangers of what they were doing on one level but on another they did not. They were blessed. They could opt to turn around at any point and return to their mansion and put this whole mad folly behind them.

So could he, if he wanted to. He could just turn his horse around and ride away. It was a thought that sometimes crossed his mind. Only it was not possible. He had sworn an oath to do this and his soul would be peril if he did not. If he had a soul, he thought sourly. He had seen enough in his lifetime to make him have doubts of the faith he had been taught as a boy and had sworn to serve as a man.

He would kill the demon if he could for any number of complex and individually insufficient reasons. He wanted revenge for the people Razhak had killed. He wanted to correct his own fault in letting the demon escape in the first place, and if truth be told, he wanted to kill the demon out of spite and jealousy.

Razhak had seen truly into his heart when he had spotted that. He wanted the demon dead because it was unfair that it should live and wreak havoc when he must die and walk into the Lands of Dust, if such lands there were. By killing Razhak, he would build his own small, secret monument. He would end the life of something that had existed since the dawn of history. He would achieve something, even if that thing was a negative.

He knew when he looked at things in this light that simple vanity was the real reason he had agreed to let Luther and Olivia come. He wanted witnesses. He wanted it recorded. He wanted it to be set down in a poem that would be remembered by future generations, the only limited form of immortality he could be certain was real. He too wanted glory.

He looked again at the desert and the people and the brilliant sun over the empty land. He thought of the living city behind them and the dead city ahead.

This is glory, he thought? It did not quite seem as the epics he had read as a boy had made it to be.

"You look sad, Sir Kormak," Olivia said.

"This desert makes me feel very small."

"It does that to everyone," she said. "It is a good place for holy hermits."

That evening they set up camp amid the dunes, raising silk tents, setting watch. On the horizon, to the North a golden light glowed in the sky, the great burning stone set atop the Tower of the Sun sending out its message of light into the wastes.

"They say the ancient Solari set it there as a challenge to the Moon," said Olivia. She was sitting by the fire, on a small intricately patterned rug, drinking water from a silver cup, eating waybread and dates from a carved platter of wood. "Its light keeps her Children at bay."

"Why is it that the Children cannot endure the Sun, do you think?" Prince Luther asked. The guards, all of those who were not on watch, sat in a circle around the fire, silent as stones. "Is it because of his curse, as the legends say, or is it something else. Could it be that they are even more sensitive to its light than an albino eunuch would be? Could it be that it burns them in the same way as it burns us only worse?"

"This is my brother's pet theory," said Olivia.

"You disagree?" Kormak asked.

"It is as good a theory as any other I have heard," she said. "And it is not impossible that both my brother and the Golden Books are correct. Perhaps the Sun's curse is that the Children are sensitive to His light."

Kormak shrugged.

"You disagree?" she said.

"I don't know. I do know they are cursed. I have seen it for myself. Too long in the Sun's holy light unprotected and they die."

"Die? How?" Luther asked.

"They simply cease to be. If they have created a physical form, it disintegrates. If they are immaterial spirits, they come apart like mist in a strong wind."

"Does your sword work according to the same principle?" Luther asked.

"I do not know," said Kormak. "You would need to ask the dwarf who made it?"

"The Dwarves were the artificers of the Old Ones," said Olivia. "Who would know them better?"

Luther said, "The Ghul were servants of the Old Ones too. Why did so many of their servants rebel against them, that is what I wonder."

"Because they wanted what the Old Ones had," Olivia said. "Or they wanted their own lives to be better."

"Or they simply hated them," Luther said. "Their lives were long and the Old Ones cruel."

Luther looked at Kormak. "It seems the Ghul learned cruelty from their masters too."

Kormak thought back to the things he had seen in Razhak's mind. "I think the cruelty was always in them, as it is in all things. A deer sees a lion as cruel. A lion thinks of himself as hungry. It's all in the point of view."

"Spoken like a hunter," said Luther.

"Razhak thinks I am cruel because I hunt him," Kormak said. "I think he is cruel because he has killed people I knew. We both could be right."

"I think you hunt him because it is who you are," Luther said. "You are what you were born to be and what the world has made you."

"That's as may be," Kormak said. "But hunt him I do. And now I must sleep."

Olivia joined him later. They made love as the desert wind blew around them.

The Sun rose over the desert. Olivia was gone, returned to her tent. Even if all the men present knew what was going on, it seemed the proprieties must still be observed. Kormak donned his gear. They breakfasted, mounted up and rode on.

They were following the little that remained of an ancient road now. The workmanship was not Solari like the road that led to Sunhaven. It was more like a trench that somehow never quite filled with windblown sand. At times Kormak caught sight of the remains of ancient runes worked in moonsilver whose enchantments still kept the path clear. Most of it had been scavenged long ago but what remained was a mere film, like gold leaf, but it still held enough power to maintain a sliver of the Old Magic.

"The Old Ones built this road," he said.

"Or their servants," said Olivia.

"We walked a path they trod millennia ago," said Luther.

"Razhak trod it within this last few days," Kormak said. A small rat of fear gnawed at his stomach. What if he was too late? What if Razhak had found what he had come for and already departed, or gained so much strength he could not be killed. He reached up and touched the hilt of his dwarf-forged blade for reassurance. Anything could be killed. All it took was the right weapon. His glance wandered to Olivia and then Luther.

Why was he travelling with them? He might only be giving the Ghul more victims. His earlier certainty about wanting witnesses had vanished. The thought occurred to him that they were bait. He did not dismiss it as entirely groundless. Razhak would be burning through Scar's old body now. He would need a new one soon. Both Luther and his sister were young and fit. They were exactly the sort of bodies the demon would want.

Had he really become so cold, Kormak wondered, that he could use people he liked in this way? He already knew the answer and did not care for it.

Buildings began to appear on the rocky hills they passed. They did not have the clean lines and columns of Solari architecture. They were low built, curved, something of their shape was suggestive of eggs, of igloos, of yurts. There were a few towers and on those were domes and minarets.

Sometimes they passed statues depicting beings too beautiful and potent to be humans. Kormak wondered whether he was looking on the features of ancient Gods or living Old Ones. He suspected it was the latter.

A massive head emerged from the sand, like that of a swimmer standing in deep water. The face was long and lean, the cheekbones high, the ears pointed, the teeth its smile revealed were sharp and two of them were fangs. It was a face at once ascetic and decadent, full of strange hungers and it was possible that the being who wore those features three thousand years ago was still in the world and walking in the light of the Moon.

"Anaskandroth," Olivia said. She gestured at the head. "The Lord of the Hunt. He was one of those who besieged Tanyth all those centuries ago. His bow shot arrows of silver light and he could bring down anything as far as the horizon."

Kormak rode closer to her. "How do you know that?"

"Because I read, Sir Kormak."

"But what do you read, my lady?"

She smiled a secretive smile that reminded him of the expression on the statue's face. "Am I your lady, Guardian or do you mock me?"

"In this place, at this time, you are."

"A very qualified statement."

"I have answered your question but you have not answered mine."

"There were humans in the armies of the Old Ones who besieged Tanyth, just as there were within its walls. They were the lowest of slaves, the most common of foot soldiers, but a few were scribes. They left records and those records were transcribed. Obviously you did not pay much attention to those scrolls I sent you."

"I had only one night," he said, "and for much of it I was otherwise occupied."

She smiled again. "Excuses, excuses."

The day wore on. The Holy Sun rose hot and high and they wended their way through the desert. Bare mountains rose in the distance, giant rocks rose from the waste. The trail all but disappeared in many places to reappear when least expected. Kormak found he was glad of the company. He was a man of the far North and felt out of place in this brilliant, sun-blasted land. The shimmering haze in the air deceived the eye and made him think of illusion spells. The ancient ruins scattered around the place reminded him that this land was old and he was a mere mortal.

And yet, for all that, he was happy. Just the act of moving across the empty wilderness provided him with a sense of satisfaction. Looking on new vistas satisfied some deep hunger in his mind. Being reminded of his own mortality made him feel the small pleasures of being alive all the more keenly.

As the shadows lengthened he noticed that something was keeping pace with them. The creatures were too far away to be seen in any detail but there was something about their movements that made Kormak think of monkeys, although there was something else there, a slinking stealth that made him uneasy.

Prince Luther produced a telescope and focused it on the creatures following them. "Lopers," he said, handing the device to Kormak so that he could take a look.

Kormak raised it to his eye and twisted the bronze tube as he had seen the Prince do. He caught a glimpse of the true nature of the creatures. They moved on all fours like monkeys, but their features were like those of men. Their limbs were enormously elongated, their hands and feet ended in sharp claws. When they opened their mouths he could see that they had fangs there. Their skin was grey and unhealthy looking, their eyes reddish and bloodshot and feral.

They looked like some spawn of the Old Ones but they could not be for they were out in the Sun's light.

"What are they?" Kormak asked. It was Olivia who answered.

"According to Eraclius they were men once, cursed by the Old Ones to eat flesh and drink blood for rebelling against their masters. Amadarius claims it was the Ghul that did it. They and the surviving travellers that encounter them all agree about the drinking of blood and eating flesh. They haunt the lands around Tanyth. They seem able to go for weeks without food or drink but when they encounter prey they like to gorge."

"They attack mostly at night," Luther said. "Their sight is better then than ours. They are very hard to kill. Sorcery has given them an unnatural vitality."

"Undermen," Kormak said. He knew the Old Ones had done things to humans with their magic, changed them, made them less than human. It was one of their arts. They needed soldiers and workers that could handle holy metals and bypass Elder Signs and go out in the Sun.

A hideous half-human howling and gibbering drifted on the wind. There was an answering howl from the distance to the north and then again from the wastes behind them to the north-west.

"It's not just one pack," said Luther. "It may be an entire clan of them. If they decide to hunt us things might not go too well. We'll need to find a defensible spot for the night."

"We can keep fires burning," said Olivia. "They do not like fire."

"Few of the enemies of Men do," said Kormak.

"It is the gift of the Sun," said Luther. For once there was no irony hidden in his voice.

"I have some alchemical preparations that might stop them," Olivia said. "I will need fire and time to prepare them."

"We shall see what we can do," said Kormak.

Luther led them to higher ground on which an old Lunar temple had once stood. It had the dome pattern and the minarets, and symbols of the crescent moon were inscribed on the arches that supported the roof. Part of the dome was gone and the sky glittered through it. There was an altar-well in the centre which seemed to go down a long way into the earth. No one was particularly keen to drink from its waters. They corralled their horses in one corner of the chamber, a cave-like area which looked as if it had once held masses of worshippers.

Olivia produced a brazier and set it up in the centre of the chamber. She lit it with an application of some sulphurous smelling oil, produced flasks and packets of chemicals from her pack, and began to mix their contents in a metal beaker she held over the flame with a set of tongs.

"When I tell you to, cover your eyes. It will go badly for you if you do not." The howling of the loper pack sounded closer. There could be no doubt that they were on the trail and had caught the scent.

Kormak studied the guards closely. They were calm, stolid men and they kept their nervousness well-hidden. He had no doubt they would respond like the veterans they were when the combat came.

Luther looked pale but excited. His eyes were bright. He had obviously found the adventure he had been seeking. Kormak hoped his enthusiasm for it did not get him or anybody else killed.

He listened to the howls, watched Olivia go about her preparations and considered the fact that he might die here. The thought did not trouble or excite him the way it once had when he was young.

Death had walked at his shoulder for most of his life. He did not feel as if he was going to encounter the Dark God this night. He told himself to beware. Such overconfidence could get him killed. He had seen men die through being convinced of their own invulnerability. They had no concept that death could come to them as well as anybody else.

And suddenly the lopers were there, swarming in through the doorways and the windows, chittering and howling. Close up they looked both more and less human. Hunger glittered in their narrow reddish eyes. They raised claws long as daggers and Kormak understood why they had no trouble climbing in through the high windows. The backs of some were red bloody strips as if some of the lopers had clambered over the flesh of their kin. The wounded ones did not seem troubled.

The Prince's guard greeted them with a volley of arrows. The force of the impact knocked many of the lopers from their feet but they picked themselves up, with strange cat-like mewling sounds, arrows still protruding from their bodies. No blood emerged from the wounds.

Hard to kill indeed, thought Kormak. A man would not have been able to rise after being hit at such close range with those arrows. He fought down his own rising bloodlust and kept his position beside the Prince and his sister. He needed to keep them alive to ensure the loyalty of the warriors. They would stand their ground as long as their employers did.

The lopers halted for a second, inspected their wounded, surged around in a confused mass, then one bigger and longer and leaner than all the others barked something in what sounded like a mangled version of the Old Tongue. The lopers bounded forward, covering the ground between them and their prey in gigantic, capering leaps.

The guards met them with flashing swords. The lopers were unarmoured and the blades buried themselves in flesh easily enough but the creatures did not die from wounds that would have killed a mortal man instantly.

Kormak looked out onto a seething sea of hungry faces and thought he might have misjudged the situation earlier. They might die here, overwhelmed by a horde of unkillable, hungry man-eaters.

"Cover your eyes," Olivia said. She sounded calm. Kormak wondered whether it was wise to do so when facing so many foes, but he raised his arm anyway. There was a brilliant flash. He was vaguely aware of it through his closed lids. The lopers screamed and howled and when he opened his eyes again he saw that they were on the ground, covering their own eyes, whining and mewling with pain. Kormak stepped forward and stabbed the nearest one. Its flesh burned where the dwarf-forged blade touched and it died as a man would have from its wound. The howl it let out was long and full of agony and seemed to dismay the lopers even more.

"Cut them to pieces," said Prince Luther. It is the only way we can be certain of killing them."

The warriors did as instructed. Kormak strode among the blinded monsters, killing a loper with every blow. When the creatures eventually recovered their sight, they fled. The warriors sent arrows after them, until they were invisible in the shadows of the night.

Afterwards even the usually quiet guards seemed elated. They spoke to each other in low tones. Some of them slapped Kormak on the back, clearly reassured by his presence or that of his blade.

Olivia looked a little sick now that the danger was over. She walked up to Kormak, hugged him close, then pushed him away and looked at him. "I was not sure that would work. The light of burning skystone is said to be inimical to the Old Ones. I thought it might do something to their creations as well."

Kormak found he was smiling, glad that they were both alive. "You were correct, fortunately."

Luther walked over to join them. "An auspicious omen for our quest," he said. "We have overcome the first great obstacle."

Kormak studied the butcher's yard of dismembered lopers around them. "Let's get out of this place and find a cleaner camp."

Olivia nodded. Luther seemed distracted. He walked over to the bodies and looked at them closely as if he could not quite believe what he was seeing. Kormak wondered if he had ever been so close to violent death before. There was a wildness in his eyes now that Kormak had seen in those of youths after their first battle. Luther leaned forward, picked up a severed head and looked at it closely, as if trying to commit every feature to memory.

The Prince noticed Kormak looking at him. "I killed this one," he said. "I am considering keeping the head as a trophy."

"You might want to put it in a jar then and pickle it with salt. A rotting head is not the most pleasant of baggage to take with you on a journey."

For a moment, Luther looked as if he was seriously considering Kormak's words and then he dropped the head. "You are right, Sir Kormak. I will simply commit the look on its face to memory. I do not think I have ever seen anything so evil."

"Then you have not had much experience with evil," Kormak murmured so low that only Olivia caught his words. Kormak suspected the Prince would garner more experience of it before their quest was done.

Two days passed without any more violent encounters. The desert became even more drab and lifeless. In the distance crystal towers began to rise. In the night, strange lights shimmered, hinting at the presence of demonic entities. Lines of blue light pulsed between the towers creating a web of magic.

As they got closer a high-pitched keening whine filled the air. Inhuman voices could be heard, chanting in languages that no one recognised. No living creature was ever seen, no matter how hard anyone looked. The veteran soldiers looked more and more uneasy. Prince Luther looked more and more wild eyed. Olivia was the only one who seemed to calm. It was not that she was not worried, Kormak knew. It was just that she was better at keeping her fears concealed.

On the evening of the third day, they made camp in the shadow of one of the crystal towers. It bore some resemblance to the work of the Old Ones, but it seemed to be the product of different sensibility, one not exactly theirs. Inscribed on the crystal were strange runes, of the type that Kormak had vague memories of.

When he paused to consider them, he realised that they were not his memories but Razhak's. They seemed to be becoming stronger the closer he got to Tanyth. He had looked upon these towers before and once he had understood the mystical significance of each and every inscription. He felt that he could do so again if only he looked at them long enough and hard enough.

He felt a hand on his shoulder and he looked around to see that Olivia was looking at him. "Sir Kormak," she said. "Is something wrong? You have been looking at that pillar for ten minutes now."

Kormak came out of his reverie. He had not realised that he'd been standing there for so long overwhelmed by the fugue of memories triggered by the sight of the pillars.

"Razhak has been this way," he said. "He came this way many times. It is like coming home for him."

"We shall see to it that it is the last time he does so," Olivia said.

"Let us hope so," Kormak said.

"You have not come so far to fail now," she said. "Have courage, Guardian."

He was not sure that he could exactly explain to her what happened or that he wanted to. It was an odd thing to have the memories of a demon inside his mind. He wondered if this had ever happened to any Guardian before. It most likely had. There were very few things new in this world.

Even as they stood there looking at each other, a voice spoke. The words seemed to come out of the air and it took Kormak a few moments to realise that they were emerging from the pillar itself. They had a hauntingly familiar quality and once again he felt, if only he listened hard enough, he might come to understand them. He cocked his head to one side and tried hard to concentrate. He laid his hand on the crystal and it seemed to vibrate in time to the words.

"What are these things?" Kormak asked.

"Some of the sages think the pillars channelled magical energy across the land, focused the ley lines of magic so that it made the deserts bloom and springs flow. Others think it formed a barrier against the Old Ones. Some say they were created by the Old Ones as part of their campaign against the Ghul. No one knows. So much knowledge has been lost."

"Razhak knows."

"He might be the only one left in the world who does now," Olivia said.

For a moment, Kormak felt a strange sense of sympathy with the being he hunted. What must it be like to be the last of your kind, to remember things no one else remembered, to know things no one else knew?

The voices in the air kept gibbering their incomprehensible nonsense, as if ancient spirits were trying to communicate warnings to those who could not understand.

"Those are not hills," said Prince Luther, "they are ruins."

Kormak could see that he was right. What at first glance looked like rocky hills were, in fact, piles of rubble, the tumbled down remains of gargantuan structures. They ran as far as the horizon. The city of Sunhaven could have fitted into one small corner of Tanyth.

"How are we going to find the Ghul?" Olivia asked.

"I know where he is going," Kormak said.

"You can remember that."

"The spell-engines are at the centre, at the geomantic focus of the city. I will know it when I see it."

The chief of the retainers walked over. He looked embarrassed but determined. "Sire, the men have asked me to remind you of our agreement. We have seen you to the outskirts of the lost city. They will proceed no further."

Prince Luther stared at him. "I will pay each man who accompanies us a purse of solars, imperial weight."

The soldier nodded as if he had expected this. "Dead men spend no gold, sire. And the lads have families and women. We have agreed among ourselves. But I will put your offer to them and see what they have to say. Gold can be wonderfully persuasive."

Luther nodded as if he had expected this answer. "You have fulfilled your obligations to me admirably, Benjamin. Wait for us here for three days. If we have not returned by then return to Sunhaven and tell the major domo of my house that if we have not returned in a moon, the rites must be spoken in the family crypt. My father should be informed. He may wish to preside over them."

Benjamin nodded. "It shall all be done according to your wishes, sire."

He stumped away. Luther looked at Kormak. "It seems we are on our own."

"It is what you expected, is it not?"

"Yes but now the moment of truth has arrived I find I cannot quite face it with the equanimity that I expected."

"You do not need to go on if you don't want to. You have come further than most men would."

"I do want to go on," said Luther. "But I find that I am afraid."

"At least you are brave enough to admit it."

Luther laughed. "I admire your skill with the paradoxical phrase, Guardian." He looked at his sister. "How about you Olivia, will you go on?"

Kormak has the sense that if she refused to go on, Luther would stay behind also. Remaining to protect his sister would give him the excuse to do so while allowing him to retain his self-respect. Kormak had seen many men at these delicate moments before. The whole pattern of people's lives could be altered by such decisions and they came and went with such speed.

Olivia appeared to be giving the matter serious consideration but Kormak knew she had already made up her mind. "Yes. I want to see the end of this and I want to see the heart of the city."

Benjamin returned. "The lads will accompany you in return for the increased payment. They would probably have come anyway. They feel safer close to the Guardian's sword and your sister's magic."

"It is alchemy," Olivia said. "Not magic."

Benjamin's respectful nod hinted at the fact that he had no idea of the difference.

Luther deflated a little. "Well, that's it then. We go on." He sounded disappointed and afraid.

Kormak shrugged. "Mount up then and let us be away."

They rode through the streets. The city looked as if an army of giants had stormed through it, kicking down buildings, setting them alight. Some of the stonework was blackened and cracked. Statues had been defaced. Shards of broken runic crystal lay everywhere.

"This army resisted the Old Ones for centuries but the First Empire destroyed it in a year," said Luther.

"The Old Ones were not really trying," Kormak said. "It was a game they played to while away the time. They do not think or set goals as mortals do."

When the words came out, Kormak knew they were true. The knowledge was a mixture of Razhak's and his own.

"They were thorough," said Olivia.

"Solareon brooked no opposition to his rule." Kormak said. "He was a proud, cruel man."

"But a great one," said Luther.

"A great mage certainly," said Olivia. Her tone made it clear that one had little to do with the other. "Possibly the greatest human mage of all time."

"And chosen by the Sun as well, filled with the Light. How else could he do what he did?"

"An army of warriors and an army of mages always helps achieve military goals," said Kormak. "And he had both."

He studied the ruined streets all about him. The destruction was on a titanic scale but it had all happened long ago. It was like looking at a stage long after the actors had left. Cataclysmic events had occurred here but in a time so remote as to make them unimportant.

Incongruously, a Solar centurion's helmet sat on top of a ruined column, as if its owner had just set it down hours ago and would return to reclaim it.

"You are smiling, Sir Kormak," said Olivia.

"Just when I think I understand something, it slips from my grasp," he said.

"It is often the case," she replied. She glanced around them, shivered and pulled her cloak tight although it was not cold. "This place is not what I expected."

"It has a certain shattered grandeur," said Luther.

"Yes, but it is remote, unconnected to our world."

"The builders of this city were not men," said Kormak.

"The destroyers were," said Luther. He sounded at once exalted and appalled by the idea. "We are used to the idea that we live in the shadow of titans, that we are less than the Old Ones but men did this . . ."

"The First Empire was as powerful as any of the Nations of the Old Ones," said Kormak. "Much was lost when it fell."

"Oh, I know, Sir Kormak but it is one thing to know something and another to feel the certainty of its truth."

At that moment, the look in his eye reminded Kormak of the old hermit, Luther's father. It was easy to see the connection of blood between the two of them.

They came to the junction of two huge streets. A statue still stood. It was blacked and defaced which gave it a demonic look. At first it seemed to resemble a man, but the proportions were wrong. It was broader and the limbs were thicker. The features were doughy, the eyes round pools in the face, the nose tiny, the nostrils mere slits. There was something suggestive of the face of a cat about it.

"That is what the Ghul originally looked like, I am guessing," said Luther.

Kormak nodded. Again he had that nagging sense of familiarity, as if he could put a name to the face if only he tried hard enough to remember. For him this place was doubly haunted, by the ghosts of ancient wars and the ghosts of Razhak's memories. There was a strange sense of homecoming about all of this.

More memories came back, of great herds of humans who served the Ghul, who had thought it the greatest of honours to be possessed by them, that somehow they became god-like themselves by surrendering their bodies. In a way, they had achieved a shadow of immortality by doing so. Razhak had absorbed their memories as he stole their flesh, and thus the pretence of humans joining the ascendant Ghul had been maintained. It was a cruel world, Kormak thought, and always had been.

Ahead of them now was a massive crystal dome, it sat atop a colossal structure that not even Solareon's armies had been able to destroy. Within it lights flickered and glowed. As they approached, the air vibrated and there was a scent of ozone.

"The Temple of the Immortals," said Kormak and suddenly he knew the real reason the First Empire had spent so many lives taking this place. Solareon and his men had believed that the secret of eternal life had lain within. Obviously they had been disappointed by what they had found or the world would have been much different.

"We have found what we were looking for," said Luther. And what exactly was that, Kormak wondered?

They passed through a gigantic arch into the cool shadows of the temple's entrance. The damage here was less than that in the rest of the city.

Why was that, Kormak wondered? Was it because it was further from the walls or for some other reason. Why would this place have been spared when the rest of the city had been ravaged? It was bigger, bulkier, even more enormous than the structures around it but that could not be the only reason.

"Solareon spared it because he intended to come back and try one last time to fathom its secrets," Olivia said. Kormak had not realised he had spoken aloud. That was worrying. Something about this place was getting to him. Normally he had more self-control. "He died in the Draconian Wars before he could do so. So Eraclius writes anyway."

"It is probably just as well," Kormak said. "The world would have been very different if he had uncovered the secrets of the Ghul."

"Yes, it might have been better," said Luther. Kormak looked hard at him.

They emerged from the entrance archway into a glittering hall. It was full of crystal pillars. They were milky and translucent except where their surfaces were scored by glowing runes. Those inscriptions seemed to float on their shimmering surfaces. Once more the air hummed with babbling insane voices. In the distance other sounds could be heard like the rumble of a waterfall, weird ephemeral music, the roaring of great angry beasts. Somehow it all blended together and was obviously all part of the same process even if Kormak could not work out what the connection was. The areas between the pillars were marked by shadows that were not quite shadows. They shimmered oddly and moved in a way that was entirely unconnected with the glow of the lights in the hall. They moved in a furtive sneaking fashion as if they had a life of their own.

"Stay within the light," Kormak said. "I do not like the look of those shadows at all."

"I was about to say the same thing," said Luther. His voice sounded subdued and quiet through all the background noise although Kormak knew he was shouting. A hissing, crackling sound came from a distant corner of the chamber, lights flickered and danced.

"No one whoever visited this place recorded anything like this," said Olivia.

"It's Razhak's doing," said Kormak, recalling more of the Ghul's knowledge. "He has activated the great spell-engines. We must seek him in the Chambers of Rebirth."

A scream rang out. Kormak turned and saw that one of the men had wandered too close to the glittering shadows. It surged forward like a wave and enshrouded him. He was transformed into a statue sculpted from shadow. His flesh became dark and insubstantial, his eyes pockets of deeper darkness. He leapt towards another man and reached out and the shadow spread from where it touched and began to transform the second victim. His screams were hideous.

Kormak stepped forward between the shadowman and his next victim. He lashed out with the flat of his blade. Where it touched the shadow receded but the man it had enveloped dropped to the ground. Kormak twisted to strike the second with the same result. The shadows that had surrounded the men skittered away, vanishing as if afraid of the touch of the dwarf-forged blade.

Kormak touched the victims. Their skin was grey. Their flesh was cold. Their eyes were open but there was no life in them or any sign of intelligence. Even as he watched they lost all animation. It was plain that death had taken them. Kormak looked over at Prince Luther. The Prince made the Elder Sign of the Sun with his hand. It was plain they were both thinking the same thing. The soldiers were paying a high price for their purse of gold.

They moved towards the centre of the chamber under the glittering dome and Kormak saw that there was a great well there, exactly where he had expected to find it; a ramp spiralled downward around the edge of the well, disappearing deep below the earth. It looked as if a god had tried to bore a hole right through to the centre of the world. Kormak remembered Luther's story of demons imprisoned beneath the surface of the land and wondered if the Ghul had been trying to release them. Razhak's memories hinted otherwise but infuriatingly told him nothing more.

All around the glowing shadows danced, the infernal voices sounded, lights shifted around the crystal pillars. For all the tremendous activity of the place, Kormak was filled with a sense of wrongness, of the idea that this was not how things were supposed to be here.

"I suppose we are going to have to go down," said Luther. He did not sound enthusiastic although his eyes were wide with wonder and fright from contemplating their surroundings.

"You suppose correctly," said Kormak. He strode down the ramp. The two siblings followed him. The soldiers marched fatalistically in their wake.

They made their way downwards, every step illuminated by the light pouring through the great crystal dome. They passed entrances that led to other tunnels which ran off as far as the eye could see. A city as great as the one on the surface was buried here, Kormak realised.

He wondered if it was as ruined as the one above. He did not have time to break off and explore and find out. His borrowed memories told him that he needed to keep going. He knew what Razhak sought and where it had to be. The activity all around told him that the Ghul was close to getting what he had come for. Other recollections told him that there were strange and deadly weapons buried here and other defences Razhak might call on if threatened.

Benjamin and the remaining soldiers moved along cautiously. Some of the warriors had bows in their hands, others had swords. The ones with the blades stood ready to protect the ones with the ranged weapons in case of surprise attack. Prince Luther had his sword out. Olivia's hand toyed with something inside the pouch she carried. She clearly had other surprises for any attackers.

The lights flickered. The air vibrated. The ground shook, not as if it had been hit by an earthquake but rather as if it were a monstrous gong being struck by an invisible but inexorable hammer. Kormak got the sense that the whole ancient city was coming awake.

He knew that Razhak had something to do with that.

After long hours of walking they reached the bottom of the well, passed through an arch and entered another great open space. This one was lined with more crystalline towers between which chain lightning flickered.

Around the edges of the space were glass jars full of milky fluid. As he got closer Kormak saw that there were things floating within the fluid, the shrivelled corpses of the ancient race to which he knew Razhak belonged. The jars had been cracked and discolouration around the floor of many of them told Kormak that strange chemicals had leaked onto the ground.

In the centre of the chamber a huge platform stood supported on a crystal pillar. At the edge of it was a massive pulsing crystal; beside it stood Razhak, still wearing the body of Scar. The flesh was starting to peel from the huge orcish frame in places. The sight of him made the soldiers flinch.

In his hand, he held something that looked like a spear tipped with a glowing crystal that resembled that from which the glowing pillars were made. The air around Razhak shimmered with light.

"Guardian!" The voice came from all around, seemingly part of the vibrations in the air. Kormak felt it rumbling within his chest as well as heard it with his ears. "You have arrived at last. And you have brought me some more vessels. I am grateful. I had thought I was going to die here, but there is yet a chance for me to live."

"Today is the day your life ends," Kormak said. He was not sure whether his shout could be heard above the noise of the spell-engines but Razhak seemed to have no trouble understanding him.

"I had thought so too, Guardian. Our ancient enemies did their work well. They have broken the god-machines. They have smashed the spell-engines. They no longer function. I had thought to remake myself, to reweave the thread of my existence but it cannot be done. Your insect forebears destroyed things they cannot even begin to comprehend out of malice and envy. Of course, you understand that all too well, don't you?"

Kormak took in what the Ghul was saying. Razhak had no way of strengthening his spirit-fires. He was as mortal in his own way as Kormak now. He might be able to leap bodies and steal part of their energy but he could not find enough energy to stave off extinction indefinitely. In fact, if they left now, he would simply starve as he burned through the remaining life energy in Scar's body.

Or perhaps that was what he wanted them to believe. Perhaps it was not so. Perhaps he had different reasons for saying this. Kormak could not take the chance of letting him escape. Razhak laughed. There was a tinge of madness to it as well as the alien mirth of one who had never been a man.

"I am going to kill you, Guardian," he said. "You have hounded me too long. I am ending this now. I will slay you if it's the last thing I do. You have, you will be pleased to know, reduced me to your own level."

He raised the spear. Chained lightning danced around its tip. Kormak pushed Olivia and Luther into the shadow of a pillar as a bolt of pure electrical energy leapt at the spot where they had been. Sparks erupted where the surge of power struck. One of the soldiers stood there watching as the lightning came closer. It touched him. He screamed, eyes opening wide, skin turning briefly white and sloughing away. In a moment, only a blackened corpse in partially melted armour stood there.

Other soldiers sent arrows streaking towards Razhak. As they got close to him, lightning streaked from the spear and they burst into flame at the tip. The stink of ozone assaulted Kormak's nostrils, its hot metallic tang making him want to gag. Two more thunderclaps sounded, two more flickers of lightning lashed out, two more soldiers died. The rest scurried for cover. Razhak's laughter rang out.

"Hiding, Guardian? Where is your confidence now? It's not so easy when your prey fights back, is it?"

Kormak squeezed his eyes shut for a moment. He was still dazzled from the flash and he could see the after-image even through his closed lids.

From cover, the soldiers started to shoot arrows again. Kormak risked a look and saw the same thing happen as before. He felt Olivia pressed against his side.

"We can't kill him with bows," Kormak said. "We need to get closer."

"It's not possible," Olivia said. "That lance will kill you before you get up the ramp. Those amulets won't protect you either any more than they would protect you from a lightning strike."

Kormak knew she was right. "There's not a lot we can do," he said. "Perhaps wait until the weapon's power is discharged."

"That might take a while," she said. "It seems to be drawing it from the spell-engines. We could all be dead by then."

"So you don't want to stand and fight, Guardian!" Razhak bellowed. "How unlike you. Must I come looking?"

"Can you use a bow?" Olivia asked.

"Indifferently," Kormak said. She dived from cover, picked up the bow that had been dropped by one of the dead guards and rolled into the shelter of a nearby pillar as another bolt came crashing down where she had been. Somehow she had managed to grab an arrow too. As Kormak watched she broke of the metal head, leaving only splintered wood. She stepped out, aimed and fired.

Kormak looked and saw that the arrow now protruded from Razhak's breast. The Ghul shrieked in pain. Olivia stepped to where

Kormak stood. "It's the metal arrowheads. The lightning is drawn to them as it is drawn to a lightning rod. Without them to draw the bolts, the arrow can get through."

She shouted to the soldiers. "Break off your arrowheads, use only the wood of the shafts and you can kill him."

A few soldiers took aim and let fly from around. Some of them panicked and did not remove the arrowheads, a few arrows clattered into the mechanism around Razhak, one bounced off his chestplate, another bit home into his flesh. The Ghul stepped away from the edge of the platform, clearly rattled. The soldiers kept up a rain of arrows on where he had been, clearly heartened by their success.

"Well reasoned," Kormak said to Olivia. He leaned forward, kissed her, drew his sword and raced for the ramp. He was surprised to find Prince Luther running beside him.

"Go back," Kormak said.

"I will see the end of this," Luther said. There was no time for Kormak to argue with him or force him back so he kept running, heart racing, fearful that the Ghul would reappear with his deadly weapon at the ready and cut them down.

They stormed up the ramp and found themselves in the shadow of the gigantic, glowing spell-engines. Razhak was nowhere to be seen. Between the ancient machines a corridor ran back into the gloom. Kormak took up a position on one side of it. He did not want to run directly down it. He would be too easy a target in the confined space.

Arrows clattered down around them. One of them, lacking an arrowhead passed through Kormak's cloak.

"Stop shooting," Prince Luther shouted. "You'll hit us!"

The rain of arrows slackened and ceased.

"Thank you," Luther shouted, with some irony. He looked over at Kormak. "What now?"

"Walking down this corridor is death," Kormak said. He looked at the great engine. There were handholds in the side. "We go over."

He started to climb until he reached the top of the engines. The air was warm and dry and the ozone stink greater. Chain lightning danced overhead and each flicker made him flinch in case it diverted itself downwards and through his body. He looked around. The top of the engines were complex patterns of machinery and crystal. He had vague memories of this being the place where the Ghul had been created, had become bodiless, reached out to become more than mortal and less than they had been.

He raced along the top, heading towards the centre of the plinth. Ahead lay a gap between two great mechanisms. He sprang across it, had a view of the surface far enough below so that a fall would break his back. He ran on, ignoring the fear in his gut, came to another gap, sprang across again and raced to the edge of the giant spell-machine, looking down.

Razhak stood below, in the shadow of a vast spherical crystal within which chained lightning roiled. He was slumped in a metal throne, the spear across his knees, trying to bind his wounds with strips torn from his shirt. It struck Kormak as oddly sad that a life measured in ages and marked with flights of cosmic evil should be reduced to this. If he had brought a bow, he could have finished him from here.

Heavy breathing beside him told him that Prince Luther had caught up. "An exciting little steeplechase," he said. He glared down at Razhak. "He is still armed."

Kormak nodded. "We go down the far side of this machine where he cannot see us."

They moved to the far edge and descended with Kormak in the lead. He was very aware of the Prince clambering down above him. If Luther fell, he would sweep Kormak to the floor as well.

Kormak moved up to the corner of the spell engine and glanced around. Razhak still sat there. He had finished binding his wounds and now glared around him like a beast at bay. He looked unutterably weary. Kormak quashed the brief strange flash of sympathy he felt. Razhak had cut down those soldiers without thought. He deserved nothing better himself.

Kormak edged from the shadows, blade held ready. If only he could reach Razhak before he turned, he could strike of the Ghul's head without interference. He padded forward and then heard the sound of a sword being drawn behind him. Razhak's head turned, he raised the lightning-spear.

Kormak desperately threw himself to one side as Razhak raised the weapon. Lightning flashed. There was a sound of screaming from behind Kormak. Prince Luther would be writing no more poems. The twisted remnants of his sword, dripped from his hand. Charred flesh had peeled away to reveal white bone beneath.

Kormak moved around the outside of the mechanism holding the great crystal sphere. He was edgy as a cat. Razhak was expecting him now and any moment he might come face to face with the Ghul and his terrible weapon. He keyed himself up to strike instantly. He knew he would only have a heartbeat in which to act.

"It's just you and me now, Guardian," said Razhak. His voice sounded loud and surprisingly close over the hum of the spell-engines. "Soon it will only be me. A pity about the boy. A good body. I could have made use of it, as I have made use of the others you brought me."

Kormak kept his mouth firmly closed. He did not want to speak, to give away his position. He wondered why Razhak was doing it. Was the Ghul nervous or did it have some other reason?

"Still, there will be other bodies. You have brought me more. Very thoughtful of you."

Kormak looked at the runes on his blade. They blazed with light but that was no help. There was so much ambient magic that they could get no brighter. There would be no warning of Razhak's presence there.

"You may have saved me you know. With those bodies I can leave here, find more hosts. Perhaps one of your mages will be able to help me stave off oblivion."

It was fear, Kormak thought. That was why Razhak was talking. The Ghul was afraid. It was closer to death than it had ever been. It knew, just as he did, that its last few moments of life were coming closer. It knew also that for it there would be no afterlife. Perhaps there would be none for Kormak either despite what the Books of the Holy Sun promised.

"I don't suppose you would make a bargain with me," Razhak said. "I could teach you my secrets. I could teach you what Solareon was so desperate to learn. You could become like me."

I have no wish to become like you, Kormak thought. He moved a pace closer, paused and listened. Part of him was tempted though. Just as part of him was repulsed. He told himself the Ghul just wanted to lure him out, that it would never keep its promise, but something in the memories he shared caused him to doubt even that.

"I know you are considering it," the Ghul said. "I know your mind better than you know mine. I have had far more experience of assimilating the memories of mortals."

He took a step closer. He could see the shadow of the Ghul now, cast from where it stood. Looking beyond that down the long aisle between the spell-engines, he could see figures coming closer, Olivia and the soldiers of her bodyguard. He saw the shadow raise its spear into the attack position.

Part of him was relieved. Olivia and the men would distract the Ghul and then he would strike. Part of him shouted, "Razhak!"

The Ghul turned to face him as Kormak sprang. It tried to turn the spear to bear on him but Kormak brought his dwarf-forged blade smashing down on it, splitting the haft. His blade buried itself in Razhak's head. He thought for a moment he had killed the Ghul but then he saw the shimmering ectoplasmic form floating in the air behind it. Once again Razhak had managed to leave the body he possessed moments before death. Looking at him now, Kormak could see differences though. The ghostly form was rent and torn and appeared to be on the verge of coming apart. It swirled through the air moving towards the soldiers faster than a man could run.

Kormak could see that Olivia was leading the men forward. Her head was slightly turned as she gave a command to her nervous followers. The Ghul was going to reach her and claim one last victim.

Kormak threw his sword towards the ghost. It turned end over end through the air and caught the apparition squarely in the centre, cleaving it apart. A long, low scream only partially physical echoed through the air, as Razhak's final form disintegrated. It came apart in a shower of light and in the end left not even a shadow. The blade clattered against one of the spell-engines and then fell to the ground.

Olivia turned her head and saw Kormak standing there. She must have read something in his face. She said, "Luther?"

Kormak shook his head, walked over and picked up his sword. He had felt oddly naked without it. Olivia walked over to where her brother lay, a roasting meat smell emerged from the corpse. She looked at it for a while, removed her cloak and covered him with it.

"We can burn the body in the desert," Kormak said. "This would not be a good place to lie for all eternity."

He was thinking about Luther's father's words when they first met. The old man had been right. This way lay Death.

THE END

ABOUT THE AUTHOR

William King lives in Prague, Czech Republic with his lovely wife Radka and his sons Dan and William Karel. He has been a professional author and games developer for almost a quarter of a century. He is the creator of the bestselling Gotrek and Felix series for Black Library and the author of the bestselling Space Wolf books which between them have sold over three quarters of a million copies in English and been translated into 8 languages.

He has been short-listed for the David Gemmell Legend Award. His short fiction has appeared in Year's Best SF and Best of Interzone. He has twice won the Origins Awards For Game Design. His hobbies include role-playing games and MMOs as well as travel.

His website can be found at: www.williamking.me

He can be contacted at bill@williamking.me

Printed in Germany
by Amazon Distribution
GmbH, Leipzig